MW00674774

Ozzy on the Outside

Ozzy on the Outside

R. E. ALLEN

For the Scotts:
Sidney, Minnie, and Dorothy

Published by
Delacorte Press
Bantam Doubleday Dell Publishing Group, Inc.
666 Fifth Avenue
New York, New York 10103

Library of Congress Cataloging in Publication Data
Allen, R. E. (Richard E.)
p. cm.
SUMMARY: Ozzy's mother's death affects him in many ways, but an unusual young woman he encounters while running away to New Orleans helps him face life again.
ISBN 0-385-29741-6
[1. Death—Fiction. 2. Mothers and sons—Fiction. 3. Runaways—Fiction.] I. Title.
PZ7.A4360z 1989 88-29402
CIP
AC

Designed by Andrew Roberts

Manufactured in the United States of America
June 1989
10 9 8 7 6 5 4 3 2 1
BG

Special thanks to Wendy Lamb,
who brought out the best in Ozzy, and to
George Nicholson and Delacorte Press,
who brought in the author from the outside.

Ozzy on the Outside

Chapter 1

OZZY MILLS stood on the edge of the bathtub and looked at his naked body in the mirror. The mirror was on the medicine cabinet, and since he'd just taken a shower, it was coated with steam. Ozzy got down, wiped the mirror, then climbed up and looked again. He had been lifting weights for two weeks but he couldn't see much difference in his physique. He took a deep breath, sucked in his stomach, and glared at the mirror. Much better.

Ozzy shifted his hips to get a side view. He looked ominous. A smile crept across his face. That's how he'd look to Lisa Kholer. His parents would be in Denver, the lights would be low, she would be drunk . . . he had it all planned. He'd bring her upstairs to his bedroom, then wait outside while she got undressed and into bed. He'd take off his clothes in the hall and hide them in the linen closet. When he opened the door, the room would be dark and the light would fall across her shoulders. He'd stand there a minute, maybe sideways, so she could get a good look at him. Her eyes would be drawn irresistibly to his pulsating manhood and she'd gasp and look away . . .

"Hey, bathroom hog," his mother called from outside the door. Ozzy jumped down, slipped, and clutched wildly at the curtain rod. For a moment it held, then one end pulled free and collapsed with him to the floor.

"Ozzy?"

"I'm okay, I'm okay." He scrambled to his feet.

"What are you doing?"

"Nothing. I slipped, that's all. I'll be right out."

There was a pause, but he knew his mother was still there. He was glad he'd stuffed toilet paper in the keyhole.

"You're sure you're all right?"

"Jesus, Mom."

"Well, it's eight-thirty."

"I know."

He listened as she went downstairs. Mom was always doing that—sneaking up on people if she thought they were daydreaming. "Don't dream it, do it," she'd say. That was one reason he was going out with Lisa Kholer. The other reason was because he wanted to be a famous writer and he needed something to write about. Something like sex with a naked girl.

Ozzy inspected the damage to the curtain rod. Four screws dangled from their mounting, the threads caked with plaster. He also had a bruise the size of a baseball on his leg from where he hit the tub.

"Dumb, dumb," he muttered as he scraped the plaster from the screws. He climbed back on the tub, repositioned the rod, and pushed the screws back into their holes. He tightened them with his fingernail. It wasn't the most secure job in the world, but it would work until he got some bigger screws and did it right.

In his bedroom, Ozzy put on new clothes—his writer's outfit. He'd gotten the idea from the correspondence course he was taking, *Famous Authorship.* The idea was that you should dress in a distinctive way, something that people would remember in the future when biographers came to your hometown to find out about your early life. Ozzy's outfit was a black shirt with black pants and white tennis shoes. At first he'd thought of dressing all in white, but then he realized white was reserved for Southern writers, and Tom Wolfe had already done it. Brown was a good possibility except it wouldn't be different enough—a lot of unfamous people dressed in brown. Blue was good, but there were too many shades to keep track of. All-red or all-yellow looked fruity and would make people think he was from Las Vegas. Black was the best color. It looked ominous, there was only one shade, and it was easy to keep clean. Of course, Dad thought it looked stupid.

"People remember you for who you are," he said, "not for what you wear."

That was easy for him to say. Dad was a dentist, and nobody remembered what dentists wore. Being a famous writer was different, but you couldn't tell Dad that. He came from a long line of unfamous people.

Dad and Mom were eating breakfast in the kitchen. Dad had his usual bowl of Cheerios and sliced bananas and Mom was munching on a cinnamon roll with coffee. Dad was a tall, lanky man with gray hair and tangled, upturned eyebrows that always made him look a little surprised. Mom said he looked like a friendly forest ranger, which was why his patients trusted him.

"Well, you can't drive," Dad was saying, "if you don't have a license."

"I *can* drive," Mom said. "It's just against the law if I don't have a license."

Mom was the smallest one of the family. She had flyaway blond hair that was beginning to gray and intense brown eyes. She sat with one foot beneath her, leaning forward, chin raised, holding the coffee cup in both hands.

"What's wrong?" Ozzy asked. Dad looked up and shook his head. "Nothing, nothing."

"Just the usual small-town stupidities," Mom said.

Dad frowned. "Stupid or not, Gwen, it's the law."

"A stupid small-town law."

"Why? What happened?"

"Your mother got another ticket."

"For speeding?"

Mom said, "For making the same right turn I've made a thousand times before."

Ozzy remembered last year when Mom ended up with so many speeding tickets and illegal U-turn tickets that they suspended her license for ninety days.

"Are you going to lose your license again?"

Mom gave him a sour look. "No, I am not going to lose my license again, thank you."

"You will," said Dad, "if you keep making right turns against the light."

Ozzy went to the refrigerator and began searching the shelves while Mom complained.

"I'm not going to waste my life waiting for some stupid light to change when there's no traffic for fifty miles in either direction . . ."

"Obviously there was a policeman."

"In a parking lot half a block away. He wasn't even real traffic."

Ozzy said, " A real policeman, though, huh Mom?"

"Listen, you—" she began and then noticed that he had the refrigerator door open. "Ozzy, don't let all the cold air out."

"Is there any pie left?"

"On the bottom shelf. Wrapped in tinfoil."

The Timberline Tours phone rang, and Mom went to answer it. Timberline Tours was the name of the business that Mom ran from the house. She did it partly to keep busy and partly to make money, but mostly so she could travel all over the world for free. She had to take a lot of retired people along with her, but Mom had a high tolerance for old people.

Ozzy cut himself a piece of pie and and sat down.

"So," Dad said, "Mom tells me you're going out with the Kholer girl tonight."

"We're going to a movie," Ozzy said as casually as he could. He kept his eyes on the pie so Dad wouldn't see the lust in them.

"What's her name? Lisa?"

"Yeah."

"She's the one who had the baby, isn't she?"

"Uh, yeah, I guess so."

Ozzy had hoped that Dad hadn't heard about Lisa's baby, since she'd gone away to Denver to have it, but Capitol was a small town, and everybody knew everything about everybody else, especially when it came to illegitimate babies.

Dad folded his napkin and casually placed it on the table. "So, uh, how long have you known Lisa?"

"She's in my Arts and Crafts."

"I don't think I've ever met her."

"Hmm."

"I don't think your mother has, either."

"Hmm."

"So what movie are you going to see?"

"I don't know. I mean, I thought I'd let her pick."

"Tell you what. Why don't you bring her by afterward?"

"Bring her by? You mean here?"

"Your mother and I have never met Lisa."

"But you'll be in Denver."

"Change of plans. Dave Wannamaker has to go to Chicago, so we won't be seeing them until after Christmas."

"You'll be *here* this evening?"

"Looks that way, so if you and Lisa want to stop by, maybe for a ginger ale nightcap . . ."

Ozzy stopped listening. His first big life experience was going down the tubes right before his eyes. The champagne hidden in the Apple computer box, the new "Bolero" tape, the red and blue lightbulbs, not to mention the Trojans he'd driven all the way to Boulder to get. Boulder was where they had the University of Colorado, so all the drugstores were familiar with young guys coming in to buy rubbers. Ozzy had also bought a spiral notebook and a tube of Crest toothpaste so that his sexual obsession wouldn't be too obvious. And now it was all for nothing.

Dad started telling him about an exhibit at the university in Boulder, some new discovery about how Peking man and Java man got together in Australia and became aborigines. Ozzy barely heard him. He was thinking about Ernest Hemingway and wondering what Hemingway would do with Lisa Kholer to make a unique sex experience if he didn't have a bedroom.

"So what do you think?" Dad asked.

"About what?"

"The exhibit. Do you want to go this weekend?"

"I thought we were cutting a Christmas tree."

"That's Saturday. I mean on Sunday. The exhibition's open twelve to six. What do you say?"

"I don't know."

"It's fascinating work, paleontology. Like finding time capsules, blueprints of how we developed. Maybe you'll get interested in paleontology."

Dad cocked his head to one side, and Ozzy realized where the conversation was headed. He got up and took his dishes to the sink.

"Dad, I already told you, I'm going to be a writer."

"A newspaper writer?"

"A book writer."

"At least with newspapers you could deal with real people, real events, the real world."

"Those are just facts, Dad. Facts tell you nothing. I want to depict the truth of human existence. It's like Mom says, 'The unexamined life is not worth living.' "

Dad frowned. "All I'm suggesting is that you keep your options open."

"They are, don't worry."

Ozzy grabbed his books, waved to Mom, and whipped out the front door. Ever since he'd decided to become a writer, Dad had been coming up with career options, hoping he would change his mind. Dad didn't think much of *Famous Authorship.* Ozzy overheard him talking to Mom about it one night. They had come back late from a dinner party, and Ozzy was still awake. When he heard his name, he opened the bedroom door and listened.

"He looks like a junior Dracula," Dad was saying.

"You didn't say that?"

"I didn't think of it."

"Don't you dare say that. He's finally interested in something, so you should be supportive."

"He's interested in being a celebrity, that's all."

"If he's talented, why not?"

"Because it's putting the cart before the horse. *Famous Authorship,* Gwen—*famous.* I mean, really."

"Would you rather he be another of life's nonentities? Another faceless tadpole swimming in the crowd . . . ?"

"Oh, Gwen."

There was a pause and the clink of a clothes hanger. Then Mom said something that Ozzy couldn't quite hear and Dad said, "You promised you'd stop pushing."

"I'm not pushing him," Mom snapped. "Don't say that."

Dad didn't answer, and Ozzy knew he was letting Mom cool down. After a moment they shut the bedroom door and when they started talking again, their voices were muffled and Ozzy couldn't make out the words. He shut the door and lay down on the bed. In a way he could see Dad's point. *Famous Authorship* wasn't the best title in the world, but what could you expect? Most of the good names were already used, and how many people would want to read a book called *Writing to Fail*? The only reason to do anything was to be good at it. Mom always said, "Be the best or be the worst but don't be mediocre." Ozzy felt the same way. If he ever looked in the mirror and saw a mediocre person staring back at him, he'd shoot himself.

It was a crisp, cold day with a hint of snow in the air. To the west, the Rocky Mountains rose like a wall, the green foothills and gray peaks and white ridges of the Continental Divide all piled one on top of the other. That was the great thing about Colorado—the mountains. The mountains and the air. Otherwise, it would just be Kansas.

Ozzy stepped off the sidewalk and walked in the gutter kicking dead leaves. Kicking dead leaves was how he solved problems, and the problem he had now was where to take Lisa Kholer. The one place he didn't want to take her was the backseat of Mom's car. That wasn't the way famous writers did things. Famous writers found Indian girls on the shores of Lake Huron or honeysuckle Southern girls on pink front-porch swings or truckstop waitresses with perfect teeth who took them to house trailers and said, "You sure look young, honey," as they unhooked their bras. The *really* famous writers didn't even stay in America for their sex experiences. They went to Paris and found artists' models with names like Astride and Odette who bit their ears and moaned in French while concierges downstairs looked up at the ceiling and smiled. Famous writers did exotic things that they could write up in books and get famous for. That's why he had to do something exotic with Lisa Kholer; then he could change her name and immortalize her along with Madame Bovary and Cleopatra.

He was still walking and kicking leaves when Mom came jogging up behind him. She was wearing a maroon sweatsuit that said Property of Alcatraz Prison. When she reached him, she slowed down but kept jogging in place beside him.

"So where is it?"

"What?"

"Your most memorable event."

"I haven't done it yet."

She was talking about his first assignment for *Famous Authorship:* Describe the Most Memorable Event of Your Life. He had figured it would be the date with Lisa, but now he would have to find something else.

"I thought it was due this week."

"No."

"It's not?"

"It's not like school, Mom. You can do them anytime you want."

As they passed under a tree, something caught Mom's eye. She stopped, grabbed Ozzy's arm, and pointed upward. "Look. Look at that, a hummer."

He followed her finger to where a hummingbird hovered, moved suddenly sideways, and hovered again.

"What's she doing here this time of year? Hey, little one," she called. "It's December. Why aren't you safe and warm in Brazil?"

As if it had heard her, the hummingbird disappeared in a quick blur. Mom turned to Ozzy. "The poor little thing is all out of season. She's going to freeze to death."

Ozzy shrugged. "They know how to take care of themselves."

"I hope so."

They crossed the street and Mom changed the subject. "Promise me one thing," she said. "Once you start, you won't quit, okay?"

"Start what?"

"That writing course. If you're going to do it, stick to it—"

"I will."

"—and don't stop halfway through. Don't be like Sissy and Lance."

"I won't." Sissy and Lance, his sister and brother, were the twin disappointments of Mom's life.

"All or nothing, promise?"

"Mom . . ."

"I know, it's your life, it's up to you what you want to do."

"I'm not going to quit."

"Don't promise me; promise yourself."

The football field appeared in front of them, and Mom glanced at her watch. "You're going to be late."

"No, I'm not."

"Want to bet?"

Ozzy checked his own watch. He had about two minutes to make it to class. "What kind of odds?"

"Odds!" Mom stopped jogging and pushed back a strand of hair.

"Two to one? My five against your ten?"

"Well now, let's see." She scratched her head and spoke with exaggerated slowness. "If them odds is two to one and you puts up five and I puts up ten . . ."

Ozzy grabbed her arm. "A deal, right?"

". . . and five and ten makes fifteen . . ."

"Will you cut it out? A deal or not? Come on."

She dropped back into her normal voice. "It would be worth it just to see you run."

"It's a deal?"

"Sure."

Ozzy clutched his books and took off in a mad dash across the field with Mom following close behind. The white yardlines flashed past diagonally under his feet and then the dirt of the oval track and the pavement leading to the north gate, where finally he stopped and turned around.

"Ten dollars," he yelled as Mom came up. "Pay up tonight."

Mom nodded, but she had something else on her mind. "You're the special one, Ozzy. Don't let me down."

Before he could respond, the bell caught him short. He turned and ran across the driveway through heavy double doors into the empty hallway. The bell stopped ringing and he jogged to class, his tennis shoes squeaking on the polished linoleum floor.

Chapter 2

"I WAS AFRAID you got sick or something," Lisa told him when he got to class. First period was Arts and Crafts, and Mr. Jelnick, the teacher, never marked him tardy because he thought Ozzy had artistic temperament.

"So what happened?" Lisa wanted to know.

Ozzy shrugged. "Nothing happened. I was just late."

Lisa followed him to the drill press. Her project was a laminated plastic lamp, and Ozzy was helping her by drilling a hole in the base.

"God, I was so worried. About tonight and everything . . ."

Ozzy had no idea why he liked Lisa Kholer. She wasn't his bodily type, for one thing, being on the plump side from the neck down. And her personality wasn't anything that would make Zelda Fitzgerald jealous. The best part was her face. Lisa had luxurious-type brown hair, big Bambi eyes, an okay nose, and really full lips. She was shy and didn't run with any particular crowd. Lisa was an outsider, like him, only she didn't realize it as much.

There was a time when Ozzy dated another shy girl, Sally Hodges. She was thin and almost as tall as he was, and during junior high they were mostly friends. Then, last year, Ozzy fell madly in love with her. They started dating and got as far as French-kissing, but the more passionate he got the more Sally seemed to pull away. Then she took a drama class and got all involved in painting scenery and running around with the Thespians. Ozzy sent her candy and stuck notes in her locker and stood at night in the alley watching through binoculars while she ate dinner with her family, but nothing he did could reverse the course of their breaking up.

Lisa said something, but she had a soft voice and her words were lost in the noise of the shop.

"What?"

She leaned forward. "Did you figure out what movie we're going to see?"

"Sure," Ozzy lied. "But I'm keeping it a surprise for tonight."

The drill chewed its way into the red and gold plastic. Lisa watched for a moment, then leaned closer and said, "I've got a surprise, too."

"You do?"

"I had to fight with Mom, but I got it."

"What is it?"

"I shouldn't tell you." She gave him the kind of secret smile that Mom and Dad sometimes exchanged when they thought nobody was looking. Ozzy had an inspiration: Lisa was on the pill, that's what it was. She was on the pill and her mom found out and tried to stop her. He imagined them at the breakfast table, Lisa holding a glass of orange juice and her mom trying to pull it away from her mouth so she couldn't swallow the pill. "I'll tell your father in Omaha," her mother screamed, but Lisa took the pill, anyway. She wanted a special sex experience as much as he did. Ozzy smiled to himself and turned back to the drill.

"It's a new sweater," Lisa said quickly.

"A what?"

"The surprise. It's a new sweater."

"Oh."

"It was really expensive and Mom didn't want to get it, but I told her it would be an early Christmas present, so finally she did. She put it on her credit card, though, so Daddy will have to pay for it."

"I thought they were divorced." Ozzy cranked down hard, and the plastic began to vibrate beneath his hand.

"They are, but Daddy has to pay the credit cards. That's what they agreed."

"Your mom had a good lawyer."

Lisa shrugged. "Daddy paid for him, too."

The plastic base whipped out of Ozzy's hand as the drill punched through the other side. Lisa jumped forward. "Are you hurt?"

"Come on." He gave her a disgusted look and turned off the press. The plastic base spun to a stop and Ozzy worked it free. The hole was a little ragged, so he turned it upside down and ran the drill through again. Then he brushed off the shavings and handed it to Lisa.

"I hope you like the sweater," she said in a small voice.

"I will." What he was really going to like was taking the sweater off and putting his hand on her breast.

Ozzy went to his locker and got his project, which was a plaster ashtray in the shape of a tooth. It was a Christmas present for Dad, but it needed a lot of sanding, so he put on goggles and took it over to the grinding wheel. A cloud of white powder rose around him as he worked, but he knew Lisa was watching him from across the room. She was always watching, ready to catch his eye and smile and shake her luxurious-type hair like a Clairol commercial. It had been that way ever since Grandpa Mills died and Ozzy missed a day of school to go to the funeral. When he came back, nobody said anything but Lisa. She waited three days and then gave him a Hallmark card showing angels and cherubs flying Grandpa to Heaven. It was a stupid card but a nice thing to do, and from then on, Ozzy helped her with her projects.

"I know I could do it myself," she always said. "But I might screw it up."

Ozzy figured she had a bad self-image from being an unwed mother who gave up her child. The funny thing was, nobody knew who the father was. Lisa wouldn't tell, and Ozzy figured it must have been a one-night stand with some rough, tough, unshaven Marlboro man. He figured Lisa was probably drunk and giddy and got carried away by feminine emotions that were shattered in the harsh light of dawn. That was another reason he didn't want to have sex in the car, in case that's where it had happened with the Marlboro man. Inside her slightly chubby body he sometimes felt that Lisa might be as sensitive as a thin, hauntingly beautiful girl, and he didn't want their sex experience to remind her of one that turned out badly. He had to find someplace different, someplace special—like Gary Grafton's research lab.

Gary Grafton was the closest thing Ozzy had to a best friend. They were both in the enriched program, which meant they were both outsiders. Gary was tall and gangly and so pale that people thought he was an albino basketball player, when he was really the most brilliant science student ever to walk the halls of Capitol High. Gary's specialty was genetic engineering, and everybody figured he'd have a Nobel Prize by the time he was thirty. He had scholarship offers from Berkeley and Duke and MIT. Gary's parents were rich and divorced and so happy to have a brilliant science student for a son that they gave him the apartment over the garage to use as a research lab. Ozzy figured all he'd have to do was move the bottles and tubes and tanks and oscilloscopes into a corner of the room and he could use the rest as a bedroom.

He went to the cafeteria to find Gary. It was lunchtime and everybody was hanging out in groups and talking about everybody else. At one table was a guy, Terry Cook, who thought he was some kind of comedian. When he saw Ozzy, he pointed his finger and yelled, "Hey, Zorro!" Then he pretended like his finger was a sword and made the sign of a *Z.* He had been doing this same routine every day since Ozzy started wearing his writer's outfit.

The other kids at the table laughed for the thousandth time, but Ozzy ignored them. It was like Mom always said, "I love individuals but loathe man in the mass." Mom hated what she called the joiners and two-legged sheep, and Ozzy felt the same way. Until he was twelve, Dad was in the Air Force and they'd moved around so much that he'd never gotten in the habit of joining groups. When Grandpa Mills got cancer, Dad took early retirement and came back to Capitol to take over his dental practice. By that time Ozzy was used to being an outsider and he made no effort to become one of the two-legged sheep. Sometimes, like when some devastating girl he'd like to know was part of a crowd, he felt lonely, but most of the time he was happy to stand outside the world's stupidity and watch.

Gary was eating his lunch at the outsiders' table in the corner near the Coke machine. Ozzy sat down and explained his idea about turning the lab into a love nest. Gary stared at him like a surprised fish.

"Move the equipment?"

"Just over to the corner of the room. Then I'll put up a blanket to create the right atmosphere."

"But I've got colloids in suspension."

"You've always got something in suspension or incubation or distillation."

"It's not a good time, Oz."

Gary was pushing his peas onto his fork with his thumb. It was always the most brilliant kids who had the worst table manners.

"Come on, Gary. I need someplace special that will live in Lisa's memory even when she's old and gray and retired in a wheelchair in Florida."

"Just use your mom's car like everybody else."

"Gary, who helped you collect water spiders? Who

drove you to Denver to pick up your megalomania fruit flies—?"

"Melanogaster."

"Who got bit holding those stupid mice so you could photograph them?"

"I realize that, Oz."

"I'm talking about romance, Gary. A date with Lisa Kholer, understand?"

Gary shifted his weight. "Why don't you take her to a cabin in the mountains?"

"Whose cabin?"

"Take her to a motel, then."

"Oh sure, the guy would call the cops as soon as he saw us. Lisa's not eighteen, don't forget."

"She's not?"

"She won't be eighteen until April. Come on, let me use the lab."

Gary took off his wire-rim glasses and rubbed the bridge of his nose. "Are you in love with her?"

"What's that got to do with it?"

"I'm trying to determine what model we're using, whether it's psychological or chemical."

"It's not an experiment, it's a favor. Will you help out or not?"

Gary replaced his glasses and a crooked smile spread across his face.

"Chemical. Your testosterone level is too high." He began laughing in a weird way that sounded more like a fish sucking air than a person having fun. Ozzy couldn't believe it. Here was this guy who was supposed to be his friend, a guy he'd helped with a hundred smelly experiments, laughing at him. He stood up, reached across the table, and shoved the palm of his hand into Gary's peas.

"Hey!"

Ozzy wiped his hand on a napkin. "Why don't you eat your food like a human being?"

"Why'd you do that?"

"I ask you a favor and all you can do is laugh at me."

"I wasn't laughing at you."

"Thanks a lot, Gary." Ozzy grabbed his books and started to leave. Gary reached for his arm.

"Wait a minute . . ."

"Forget it."

Ozzy pulled free and left the cafeteria. He was half-way down the hall when Gary came running after him.

"Wait, wait, Oz, I got an idea. An airplane. What about an airplane?"

Ozzy stopped. "An airplane?"

Gary stepped in front of him, talking quickly. "You wanted someplace different, why not an airplane? My Dad just got a new one last month. A twin-engine job with fold-down seats."

"Use your Dad's plane?"

"You can take pillows and make a bed. I'll give you the keys." The smile returned. "Just promise not to take off."

"What if someone sees us and thinks we're trying to steal the plane?"

"There's nobody around at night. Besides, the plane's in a hangar with no windows. Nobody will even know you're inside."

"An airplane . . ." Ozzy imagined flying through the clouds on automatic pilot with the seats down and

Lisa's nipples lit by the glow from the altimeter. The thought made him shiver.

Gary watched him hopefully. "It's perfect, Oz. Mating in a plane is totally unique."

"Does it have a CD player?"

"I don't know. But I've got one you can borrow."

The more he thought about it, the more Ozzy liked the idea. None of the other famous authors he'd read about had done it that way. He would be the first one.

They arranged to drive out to the airport after school to make sure everything was ready.

WHEN OZZY GOT HOME, he found Mom in the workroom throwing a pot. She did pottery mostly to relax, but some of the stuff that didn't get sent out for Christmas presents actually sold for real money down at the Flatiron Gallery. Mom sat at her potter's wheel wearing a blue smock. Her feet kept the wheel moving while she squeezed the red clay through her hands like a slow-motion atomic cloud.

"Hi, Mom. Mind if I use the car?"

She glanced up, and from her expression Ozzy knew she was upset about something. She made two fists and jammed her knuckles into the clay, turning the cone into an hourglass.

"Do you think he hates us, or do we just not count?"

"Who?"

"We're not important because we don't chew pinecones and smile at rocks, maybe that's it. Because we didn't jettison our brains, we don't count."

Mom had a habit of jumping past the beginning of a

conversation, but Ozzy knew who she was talking about now—Lance. Lance was his older brother, "the Big D," Mom called him—the big disappointment. Lance gave up a football scholarship to Gunnison College so that he could go to Stanford University in California, where he barely survived the first semester and flunked two courses the second semester. Then he was supposed to go to summer school, but he used the tuition for a trip to Mexico with some girl, and on the way back they were caught trying to smuggle marijuana. He got a suspended sentence and did community service and then moved to a commune in Canada. Ever since then, he had been "the Big D." Ozzy said, "What happened?"

Mom reached inside her smock and pulled out a postcard. "This came today."

It was a postcard made from a photograph. There was Lance, smiling like a happy bear, pushing his face close to his girlfriend, Naomi. She was sitting in bed holding a glistening, squinch-faced newborn baby. Part of the picture was covered by Mom's damp, clay-red thumbprint. Ozzy looked up. "They had a baby?"

"Look what it says on the back."

He turned the card over and read, "A new lifechild has joined the family of man and her name is Bree." That part was in Naomi's italic script. Next to it was a note from Lance. "Mom and Dad—come back soon and share our miracle."

Ozzy wrinkled his nose. That was just like Lance, acting as if he was the first person in the world who ever had a baby. The whole commune was like that, walking around in the mud, talking about themselves in soft voices like they were in church or something. He remembered last summer, when they went to visit Lance, how odd it was when this big Paul Bunyan guy with long hair and a full beard met them at the airport. Lance drove them to the commune in a dented yellow station wagon. Dad sat in front, and he and Mom were in back. On the way Lance told them that the commune had no name. "A name fixes you in time and space," he said. "We're not interested in classifications. There are no walls in the forest."

When she heard this, Mom stuck her tongue in her cheek and rolled her eyes, and Ozzy had to grit his teeth to keep from laughing.

The commune turned out to be a bunch of tar paper and Plexiglas shacks strung along the Takanakanook River. There was only one decent building, called Helio House, which was an old lodge that had been there when the communers bought the place.

"Helio House is our spatial nexus," Lance explained. "But it's off-limits to outsiders."

Ozzy was glad to be an outsider because the insiders looked like real rejects. The girls dressed like they had just stepped off covered-wagon trains and the guys were two types—mountain men like Lance or wimpy intellectuals with beards about three hairs thick. Naomi gave Ozzy a hug even though it was the first time they'd met. She had a round moon face, innocent eyes, and wore her dark hair braided. She looked part Eskimo, although it turned out she'd been born in Brooklyn.

Mom took the postcard and held it up to the light as

if looking for a secret message. "I told them they could call collect," she said. "I told Lance three times, *call collect.* But he never does."

Ozzy checked his watch. He was supposed to meet Gary, but he wanted to say something to cheer Mom up. "They don't have a phone, remember?"

"Yes they do, in that big building."

"It's only for emergencies. Lance told me."

"Having a baby's not an emergency?"

"Not like somebody dying."

"Fine." Mom stuffed the postcard back inside her smock. "Maybe they'll call if the baby dies."

Ozzy grinned. When Mom got sarcastic, it meant she felt better. "Can I use the car now?"

Instead of answering, Mom placed a forefinger on the rim of the bowl. As she pressed down, the edges began to flare. "First Lance and then Sissy. A puppy dog and a religious nut. You better not discard your mind when you leave home, Ozzy."

"I won't." And then, before Mom could get started on the subject of Lance and Sissy, he said, "You got clay in your hair."

"Where?" Mom started to reach, but Ozzy stopped her. He took the strand of hair between his thumb and forefinger and slid the clay off. "There. Now can I borrow the car?"

"Be back for supper."

"No problem."

As he backed the Toyota down the driveway, Ozzy wondered if Mom would think he was discarding his mind by having sex on the front seat of an airplane. For a minute he wished he could talk to her and tell her about it. For a minute he wished she were his friend instead of his mother, but then the feeling passed and he picked up Gary and drove to the airport.

Chapter 3

LISA'S HOUSE was hidden behind the Gasmat Service Station and looked like it had been a decent place to live in 1902, but in the meantime somebody had modernized it with stucco and striped aluminum awnings over the windows. There was a ratty-looking dog in the backyard that barked and threw itself against the chain link fence whenever somebody came up the walk. A faded piece of paper taped over the doorbell said Please Knock.

Ozzy tapped on the door, but nothing happened. He could hear a television inside, so he knocked louder, and Lisa came to the door. She was wearing a white angora sweater and tan slacks that didn't hold in her stomach as well as the blue jeans she normally wore. Ozzy suddenly wished he'd brought flowers or something to show that he was more gallant and thoughtful than the average-type person who asked Lisa for dates.

"Hi," Lisa said. "Mother wants to see you. I'm sorry."

Mrs. Kholer lay on a couch in the living room watching TV. She was a tiny, thin woman with gray hair and restless blue eyes and she looked more like Lisa's grandmother than her mother. When Ozzy came into the room, she aimed a remote control at the television and turned down the volume.

"You'll have to excuse me," she said. "I have edema of the ankles."

"No, Mother," Lisa said in a warning tone Ozzy had never heard before.

"Well, it feels like edema." She reached down and adjusted two hot-water bottles under her feet. Ozzy looked around the room and tried to find something to admire. On the mantel were half a dozen ceramic figures of German boys and girls and dogs in pale pastel colors.

"Is that a collection?" Ozzy pointed.

"Not mine," Mrs. Kholer grunted. "Winnie's."

"Winnie?"

"My older sister," Lisa said. "She lives with Daddy."

Ozzy was surprised. For some reason he always thought of Lisa as an only child. He wondered if she had any brothers who might get mad if he and Lisa had sex, but before he could find out, Mrs. Kholer started asking him questions.

"Is Ozzy short for Oswald or Oscar?"

"Osric, ma'am."

"Osric?" She put her mouth around the word as if it were a tennis ball. "Is that a girl's name or a boy's name?"

"A boy's name, ma'am."

"Of *course* it's a boy's name, Mother." Lisa tugged him toward the door. "We've got to go now."

Mrs. Kholer looked worried. "Wait, dear. Did you leave me a number?"

"I told you, we're going to a movie."

"A movie?"

"I told you."

"What movie?"

"It's a surprise."

Mrs. Kholer pushed herself up on one elbow and said with sudden vehemence, "I want to know what movie!"

Ozzy was amazed. When she was angry, Mrs. Kholer looked fifty years younger. He had a sudden vision of her as a young woman with flashing eyes and flying hair, standing in a Model A convertible, surrounded by Notre Dame football players who watched her wave a champagne glass in the air as they raced a locomotive to the crossing.

"What movie?" Mrs. Kholer demanded again. Lisa looked down at the floor, embarrassed.

"It's a foreign film, ma'am."

"A foreign film?"

"Yes, ma'am. Over at the university."

"The university in Boulder, is that where you're going?"

Ozzy wondered if Lisa was allowed to go to Boulder. He started explaining about the high-class European films, trying to make it sound like going to the opera, but the energy drained from Mrs. Kholer's face as quickly as it came, and she slumped back on the cushions.

"All right, all right," she interrupted him. "Just you be careful driving, you two."

As they left, Ozzy noticed a photograph on the wall

and he recognized her instantly—the carefree grin, the windblown hair, and dancing eyes. She was on a beach in an old-fashioned two-piece bathing suit, and beside her was a handsome Italian-looking guy with lots of chest hair. Between them were two little girls, one about five and one maybe two. Ozzy suddenly wished it were fifty years ago and he was going out with Lisa's mother before she met the guy with the chest hair.

Lisa started apologizing about her mother as soon as they got in the car.

"Forget it," Ozzy said. "I got a kick out of her."

They were driving west, toward mountains that rose in silhouette against a pink sunset.

"She can't help it. Acting that way, I mean."

"No, she was fine, really. She was great material."

Lisa looked puzzled. "Great material?"

"You know, for writing books. That's my career goal, famous writing."

"You like to write?"

"Not homework and term papers, but stuff like great literature and best-sellers."

"It sounds hard," Lisa said with a trace of awe in her voice.

"It's a great life," Ozzy explained. "You get a lot of wealth and fame, but at the same time you do a service for humanity. You dredge up the truth and show it to people through books. Things like man's inhumanity to man and the greatness of the human spirit."

"I never thought of it like that."

"Famous authors are the flashlights of men's souls," Ozzy said, quoting a line from *Famous Authorship.* "That's why it's good to experience crazy people every once in a while—" He caught himself and added quickly, "Not that your mom is crazy or anything."

"No." Lisa looked troubled. "She's not crazy."

"I didn't mean booga-booga crazy, anyway. I meant unusual crazy, like your mom being unusual with all those hot-water bottles on her feet."

"She thinks she has edema."

"She probably does have edema, somewhere or other."

"No." Lisa shook her head sadly. "She only thinks she does."

It wasn't exactly the romantic conversation Ozzy had in mind for the evening. He tried to think of something more exciting, something Ernest Hemingway might have said to arouse the passions of a young woman.

"Have you ever wanted to go on safari?"

"You mean, like in Africa?"

"Sure, in Africa. That's the only place where they have safaris. It's an African word."

"Oh."

"That's what I want to do—go on a safari and see nature in its most primitive form. All the vanishing wildlife, wild boars and giraffes and elephants. They hunt with cameras these days, but you have to carry a gun for protection, in case you get between a wild elephant and its baby and the elephant tries to trample you."

He glanced at Lisa. She was staring out the window with a troubled look.

"What's the matter?"

"Nothing." She shook her head slowly. "I just hate to see things die, that's all."

"Death comes to us all," Ozzy said in a doomed voice. "Our choice is how we meet it."

"My baby died," she said, still staring to where the mountains were fading into the night. "He had the umbilical cord around his neck."

"Your baby in Denver?"

As soon as he said it, Ozzy felt stupid. What other baby was it going to be? But Lisa just nodded.

"Kyle, that was his name. I was going to keep him, even though Mother and Daddy didn't want me to. I was going to keep him and raise him myself, but then he was born with the umbilical cord around his neck and he was dead."

"I thought . . ." Ozzy hesitated. "I heard you put him up for adoption."

"That's what I tell people so I don't feel so bad. I tell people and I pretend he's living with some nice family on a farm where they have goats and kittens and a grandfather clock and someday, when he's thirteen or fourteen, they'll tell him he was adopted and he'll come and find me." Lisa sniffed and wiped her eyes. "Sorry. It's stupid to tell you this."

"No, it's not."

"I don't know why. I guess because of your grandfather, I thought you'd understand."

"Oh, I do, I do," Ozzy said quickly.

But he didn't want to understand. Until now he hadn't thought of Lisa as having a family or being somebody's daughter. She was just Arts-and-Crafts Lisa who had babies in Denver. Finding out about her mother and her sister and the barking-dog house she lived in made her too real. Ozzy glanced over, but this time, instead of noticing the way her jutting breasts bounced when the car hit a bump, all he could see was the soft flesh under her chin and the thrust of her abdomen where it bulged under her belt. It wasn't the kind of stomach that made his hands tingle when he thought of touching it.

Ozzy felt the lust begin to drain from his body. He glanced at Lisa's breasts and tried to fantasize what they looked like, but it was no use. No matter what shape or size or color he imagined, they were Kyle's mother's breasts now, not playthings for his lustful tongue. Now that he knew the name of the dead baby, he felt like he knew Lisa too well to like her enough or dislike her enough to have sex with her. He reached over and put on a Bruce Springsteen tape, and Lisa smiled. Ozzy smiled back and turned the volume up so they wouldn't have to talk anymore.

The movie was an old French film called *A Man and a Woman,* and it turned out to be pretty sexy even though most of it was music and this guy driving a Mustang on the beach. The sexy part was the actress, Anouk Aimee, who was exactly the right bodily type—thin and French. She was always brushing her hand across her face in a lazy way that told you she was saving most of her energy for the bedroom. Ozzy fell in love with her instantly. He felt his lust return as he watched Mr. Mustang talk to Anouk Aimee.

"You need zee ride to Paree?" he asks.

"Merci, but non."

Mr. Mustang shrugs with one shoulder. "As you wish, but I go zat way . . ."

"Ah yes?" Anouk Aimee turns and looks right into the camera, right at Ozzy . . .

Lisa put her hand against Ozzy's knee. She did it casually, like it was an accident and she didn't notice, but Ozzy stiffened instantly. Then Anouk Aimee's five-foot face gave him a slow smile and his body betrayed him. He began to imagine it was Anouk Aimee sitting beside him, with her long black hair and wide lips and thin, French hand against his leg.

Anouk Aimee gets into the Mustang and they drive in the rain. Ozzy lifts his hand and lets it float in front of him, driving the car through the wet French countryside. Anouk's hand slides along his leg. Ozzy has an enormous hard-on. An accident on the highway, and Anouk turns to look. She has thin French legs. Ozzy slides a hand across to Lisa's thigh. Anouk gives him a grateful smile. When they reach Paris, Anouk Aimee dashes through the rain to her doorway. Clutching her sweater, she gives a little wave and disappears into the house.

With Anouk gone, Ozzy suddenly realized what he was doing. He froze, his eyes fixed on the screen, his hand turning to cement on Lisa's leg. He was aware of her breathing, of her perfume, of her head resting lightly on his shoulder. He could feel her hand on his thigh, dangerously near his hard-on. The thought of her touching him made him realize how animalistic his body was. He really didn't like Lisa all that much, but his body didn't care. It wanted girl-flesh and it didn't care whose girl-flesh it was. Ozzy felt primitive and powerful. He was glad he was born a boy instead of a girl.

Anouk Aimee came back into the movie, and Ozzy decided to go for it. He put his arm around Lisa, and she melted into his shoulder, her white sweater shimmering in the light reflected from the screen. Anouk and Mr. Mustang went to a hotel. Ozzy started rubbing his way up Lisa's leg, and she let her hand brush against his hard-on. He almost died. Anouk took off her blouse and pushed her elegant French breasts against Mr. Mustang's chest. Ozzy slid his hand under Lisa's sweater and touched her breast. Anouk and Mr. Mustang rolled over and over in bed, their naked backs flashing across the screen. Ozzy's hand stopped; it was Lisa's stomach he was caressing, not her breast.

Suddenly, Lisa became Lisa again, the same Lisa she had been in the car, a poor, lonely girl who trusted Ozzy and told him about her dead baby when he didn't even care that much about her. Ozzy felt disgusted and ashamed and sad. The passion drained out of him, and he pulled his arm back and sat up. Lisa thought he wanted to kiss. She turned to face him with her eyes closed and her lips half open and wet.

"We have to go now," Ozzy whispered. Her eyes opened in surprise. "I promised Dad . . ." He let the sentence hang. What could he say? What kind of an excuse was there for taking a girl home after she touched your hard-on?

"What's wrong?" Lisa whispered.

"I have to get the car back. Right away." Ozzy stood up and moved in a crouch toward the aisle. Lisa followed, confused. On the screen Anouk Aimee stared morosely over her lover's shoulder, remembering other times and other boyfriends.

"What is it?" Lisa asked in a normal voice as soon as they were outside. She looked worried, and Ozzy felt even worse because she looked worried for him.

"I'll tell you in the car."

Ozzy led the way across the parking lot, and Lisa followed obediently. He remembered a black, wiggly dog he'd once fed on the way home from school. It was a stray dog whose owners must have hit it, because every time anybody paid any attention to it, the dog would cower and roll on its back with its tail between its legs. Ozzy couldn't get rid of the dog without scaring it and now he felt the same way about Lisa. What could he say that wouldn't hurt her feelings? As they drove away, he told her he'd promised to have the car back by ten o'clock.

"But the movie doesn't get out until ten-fifteen."

"Yeah, I forgot about that."

Ozzy wheeled around a corner, shot through an amber traffic light, and headed north out of town. He had to get the evening over with. He put on the Springsteen tape and turned up the volume, but after a moment Lisa reached out and turned it down.

"It's me, isn't it?" she said in a dead voice that turned Ozzy's heart inside out.

"What do you mean? What are you talking about?"

"The reason you want to go home. It's me, I know."

"No, no, it's not you."

"It's my body."

"Hey, come on . . ."

"I'm too fat, I know."

"No way, Lisa," Ozzy said weakly. He hated it when

people guessed what was wrong with them and you had to pretend it wasn't true.

"When you touched me, I could feel it."

"It's not you," he said quickly. "It's me. I've got this problem."

"What problem?"

"Oh, just this . . . big problem. It's personal, you know."

The look of interest on Lisa's face faded. She bit her lip and turned to stare out the window. Ozzy cursed silently. He tried to remember what they said in *Famous Authorship* about verisimilitude and suspension of disbelief, but all that stuff was for writing, not for convincing fat people they were thin. And then he remembered Jake Barnes in *The Sun Also Rises.*

"It's my thing," he said. "I can't perform."

"Your thing?"

"I had this accident to my, you know—my organ."

"Your penis?"

Ozzy couldn't believe she said the word right out loud in public. It wasn't like she was a guy and they were in gym class talking about cocks or pricks or dicks or dongs or wangs. No, she was a girl and she said the real word, right there in Mom's car.

"Is that what you mean?"

"Right, right. I hurt it when I was a kid. I slid down a banister and hit this knob at the bottom."

"Really?" Lisa's expression was changing from unhappy to sympathetic.

"Yeah, it's true. They were hoping puberty would cure it, but it didn't do any good. I can't have normal relations or anything."

"But you felt hard."

"I know, but it wasn't real. It's plastic."

As soon as he said it, Ozzy realized he'd gone too far. Lisa got this hurt look and said, "You're making fun of me."

"No, I'm not."

"Yes, you are."

A car passed going in the opposite direction. In the sweeping headlights Lisa's face looked like it was made of stone.

"Hey, come on," Ozzy said. "I was just kidding around."

"Yuck, yuck."

Lisa reached forward and turned up the volume on the Bruce Springsteen tape. Ozzy drove home as fast as he could, feeling like a total turd all the way.

Chapter 4

THE NEXT DAY everybody was supposed to go to the mountains to cut down a Christmas tree. Cutting your own tree was an ancient family tradition, and Dad always made a big deal about it. He came into Ozzy's room early in the morning wearing a red plaid lumberjack's shirt and jeans so new the blue still looked wet.

"Okay, Paul Bunyan, rise and shine. Time to sharpen the ax and gas up the old chain saw."

"I'm sick."

"You're just hung over." He slapped Ozzy's foot beneath the covers. "Up and at 'em. Daylight on the swamps."

"No, really, I don't feel good."

"Not surprising, considering how *late* you got in last night . . ."

Dad raised an eyebrow, waiting for a reaction. The reason Ozzy had gotten in late was because he had waited in the car until they went to bed. He couldn't face answering questions about how the rotten evening went. And now Dad was looking at him, waiting for him to say something. When he remained silent, Dad said, "So how was it?"

"What?"

"The movie last night."

"Great."

"You had a good time?"

"Yeah."

Dad pursed his lips and nodded. "Well, remind me to ask you to tell me about it sometime. Maybe five or ten years from now, huh?"

He smiled to show he was kidding around. Dad had this compulsive habit of always trying to make everybody happy. "Our bridge over troubled waters," Mom called him. Sometimes it depressed Ozzy to see how happy Dad could be. He would never be that happy. He had too many dark urges and despicable yearnings.

"Come on, tiger." Dad slapped his foot again and went downstairs. Ozzy curled up in a ball and shoved his face in the pillow. Five minutes later Mom came in and sat down on the bed.

"Dad says you feel sick."

"Yeah, kinda." Ozzy made his voice sound uncomfortable. Mom put her hand on his forehead. She was wearing a Norwegian reindeer sweater, and he could feel the wool cuff, prickly against his skin.

"You don't feel hot."

"It's my stomach. I feel like I'm going to barf."

Mom tilted her head back and squinted at him like a hunter sighting a target. "What's the matter? You don't want to come with us?"

He looked away. "I do, but I don't feel so hot."

"Sissy's bringing Brenda."

Ozzy didn't say anything. Sissy was his older sister who lived in Denver, and Brenda was her daughter. Brenda was in that cute range between two and four, when kids are like kittens and you wish there was a pill you could feed them to make them stay that way forever.

Mom crossed her arms and gave him a searching look. "You're not in love, are you?"

"Oh, sure."

"Are you?"

"Come on, Mom."

"You can't fall in love in Capitol, Ozzy. It'll ruin everything."

"I'm not in love."

"Good, because your hormones are trying to sabotage your future. They want you to fall in love with the first pretty girl who comes along. They're the enemy, Ozzy. Hormones are the enemy. They're out to stick you in Capitol for the rest of your life."

Ozzy grinned.

"Don't laugh," she said. "It happened to Sissy."

"I know, I know."

Sissy had great potential as a concert violinist until she suddenly became an intense Catholic and dropped out of college to get married and have a child. Now she was a chic housewife in Denver. As Mom said, "Sissy traded her talent for kitchen, church, and children." She was "the Little D" and Lance was "the Big D."

"So are you protected?" Mom asked.

"What?"

"I mean, they give you guys sex education nowadays, don't they?"

"Mom!"

"Well, they do, don't they?"

"Yeah, all kinds of stuff. Don't worry about it, okay?"

"All right, but if you ever have a problem, I want you to let me know."

"A problem? Gee, Mom, what do you mean?"

"Are you laughing at me?"

"No, no."

"Don't you laugh at me," she warned. "I'm just trying to do my motherly duty."

"I'm not laughing." But he was grinning like crazy, and Mom gave him an outraged look. She reached over and began to tickle him. "You *are* laughing. Admit it, admit it."

"No—" Ozzy tried to grab her hands, but Mom kept after him.

"You are *laughing* at your *mother*!"

"I'm not."

"You are, admit it."

"Cut it out. Mom—" He reached over and tried to tickle her, but she blocked his hand and stood up.

"Oh no, you do not tickle your mother."

"You started it."

Ozzy began to come after her, but he remembered he was naked. He'd stopped wearing pajamas when he found out Jack London and Ernest Hemingway slept in the nude. He fell back in the bed, and Mom went to the door.

"Okay," she said. "You don't want to come with us. Just stay sick so the others won't feel bad."

"I'm feeling worse all the time."

"Right."

Ozzy stayed in bed until Sissy and Brenda arrived and then he got up and shuffled around the house in a bathrobe with his ski parka over it. Sissy was taller than Mom and took after Dad's skinny side of the family. She had light brown hair and gray eyes and kind of a tight mouth except when she smiled. It turned out that Peter was working over the weekend, so only Sissy and Brenda were going to help cut the tree.

"You stay six feet away from Uncle Ozzy," Sissy told Brenda. "He has germs."

Brenda's eyes widened, and she put her hands behind her back. She was wearing a gray snowsuit with fur lining, and with her blond hair and little angel's face she looked like she just stepped out of a Hallmark greeting card. It was funny because Sissy and Peter were just average-looking, but Brenda was so cute she got paid to model kids' clothes for the Denver Dry Goods catalog.

"I want Uncle Ozzy to tell me a story," Brenda said.

"He can't. He's not coming."

"Then I want to stay here."

"Don't you want to help Grandpa pick out a Christmas tree?"

"I want Uncle Ozzy to tell me a story."

"When you get back," Ozzy said. "I promise."

Telling stories to Brenda was what gave Aunt Rose the idea of sending Ozzy *Famous Authorship.* Aunt Rose was Mom's older sister, a widow who owned a lot of condominiums in Aspen and liked to attend opening-night concerts and operas in Denver. "Aunt Rose has a lot of energy," was what the family said about her. What they meant was, she had a lot of money. The last time she visited, she heard Ozzy telling Brenda a story. Later, she sent him *Famous Authorship* as a birthday present. The first chapter began:

> Have you ever imagined how wonderful God must have felt when he created the whole world in seven days? Famous authors know that feeling. They have it every day, and get well paid for it, too.

As soon as he read it, Ozzy was hooked. Until then he hadn't known what he wanted to do with his life, but as soon as he started reading, he knew. He wanted to be a famous writer. He wanted to create his own world where he had all the answers, and the characters in the book had to run around trying to figure things out. He wanted to be a god.

Famous Authorship was divided into three sections. First was "Famous American Authors," which gave previews of five dead writers: Mark Twain, Jack London, F. Scott Fitzgerald, Ernest Hemingway, and William Faulkner. It showed how these guys traveled around to exotic places picking up adventures to use in famous writing. They didn't work in factories or punch time clocks or get caught in traffic jams or anything. They just followed their creative juices and put their imaginations in their pencils.

Part 2 of *Famous Authorship* was the shortest. It was called "Elements of Famous Writing," and most of it was technical stuff like Plot and Dialogue and Character. That was where they gave you the tricks, like having one character jingle his keys all the time so that you could tell him apart from the other characters. Most of it was pretty simple. You just had to be a keen observer and practice guessing people's motivations.

The final section was called "Joining the Ranks," and this part had the FLP theory, which was the core of the book. The FLP theory was "famous life patterns," and what the authors did was put all this information about famous writers into a computer. Things like how much education they had and how many parents and wives and homes in foreign countries, and then they matched that stuff with how long it took each one to get fame and fortune. The theory was that if you want to be a writer, you should live like a writer and not like a truck driver or heart surgeon. There were topics like "Developing the Writer's Persona," "Keeping a Journal," "Dressing for Best-Sellerdom," and "Distinctive Autography." It was all very scientific because the authors, Hogarth and Ratliff, were both Ph.D. professors and very renowned in the twin fields of psychology and literature.

After the family left, Ozzy lazed around the house a while and then got dressed and went over to Gary's to return the key to the plane. As usual, Gary was in the converted biology lab above the garage, which meant that Ozzy didn't have to go through the house and make polite conversation with Gary's parents. They weren't around much anyway, since Gary's dad was an electronics wizard over at the aerospace lab and his stepmother was an artistic-type photographer who specialized in ghost towns and crumbling cabins at sunset.

"Good, good." Gary grabbed the keys like they were diamonds. "They're thinking of flying down to Santa Fe this afternoon. Wait a minute, I'll be right back."

Gary went to sneak the keys back into the house, and Ozzy wandered around the lab. It didn't look like it had ever been an apartment. Everything normal had been taken out and replaced with shelves and metal tables and test equipment. One table had about sixty Mason jars covered with cheesecloth. The Mason jars were where the fruit flies lived, and Gary's big thing was to try to manufacture an extra pair of wings through interbreeding techniques. The advantage of fruit flies over birds or monkeys was that they had space-age life cycles that ran through hundreds of generations in just a few weeks. Gary did worm experiments, too, but they took longer. The worms were in four plastic fish tanks, and Ozzy was inspecting them when Gary came back.

"So how'd it go last night?"

"Wouldn't you like to know." Ozzy made his voice happy and kept his back to Gary.

"You shot sperm?"

"All night long." He pointed to the fish tank. "Are these guys the same ones you chopped up last month?"

"No, over here. You can tell the ones that are regenerating . . ."

Ozzy smiled. It was easy to sidetrack Gary as long as you didn't mind looking at gross experiments and talking about DNA. He hung out with Gary for the rest of the afternoon so that he wouldn't have to think about what a jerk he'd been with Lisa. When he got back home, he was surprised that the car wasn't in the driveway. The whole reason Dad liked to leave early was to get back in time to watch the football games on TV.

He could hear the phone ringing even before he opened the front door. It felt like it had been ringing a long time, and when he answered, a strange voice said, "Is this Ozzy Mills?"

"Yes."

"One moment."

In the background Ozzy could hear someone on a radio: "Base, have they closed County Thirty-six?"

"If they did, they haven't told us."

"Ten-four, we're en route—"

Suddenly Sissy was on the line. As soon as he heard her voice, he knew something was wrong.

"Ozzy?"

"Where are you guys?"

"It's Mom." Her voice caught, then she went on. "She went to get the car. We didn't know . . . nobody was with her and she . . . oh, Ozzy—"

"What?"

The words came in a strangled cry. "She went off the road, Ozzy. She's dead."

He stood still, the phone turning to lead in his hand, a sick feeling spreading through his stomach, a feeling of falling, a dropping away, a rushing, roaring sound . . .

"Ozzy?" Sissy's voice came from far away. "Can you hear me? Are you there?"

He wanted to tell her to shut up, not to say anything, to wait, to let the moment freeze so that time would stand still and he could turn back the clock to morning and Mom would be on the bed and he could say, "No, Mom, don't go to the mountains today . . ."

"Ozzy? Are you all right?"

Be quiet, he thought. Just shut up.

"Are you there?"

Shut up, shut up.

"Ozzy? OZZY?"

"I know!" The words burst from somewhere deep inside him. "I know I know I know I know . . ."

He sank to his knees in the darkened hallway and waited while the world came to a slow, sickening stop.

Chapter 5

AUNT ROSE WAS THE ONE who drove Dad and Sissy and Brenda home. She came into the room with her arm around Dad, but when she saw Ozzy, she said, "You poor dear," and came to him. She wore a long leather coat over a blue silk dress, and as she crossed the room, her high heels sounded like dull hail on the rug. Aunt Rose had Mom's same intense eyes, but her hair was dyed ash blond and she wore a lot of makeup where Mom hardly wore any. When she hugged Ozzy, her perfume washed over him like a sweet fog.

Behind Dad, Sissy came in carrying Brenda, her face streaked with tears. Dad went to the middle of the room and stood staring at a painting of the family. It was from a photograph of everybody in the backyard. Mom and Dad were sitting down, with Lance and Sissy standing on either side of them and Ozzy between them. The original photograph had houses in the background, but the artist had changed the painting and put in mountains so that it looked like they were sitting in the wilderness somewhere.

"He doesn't know," Dad said in a hollow voice.

Aunt Rose went to him and took his arm. "Here, Frank, sit down."

"He doesn't know."

"Who?"

"Lance. Nobody called him."

"I'll call him," Sissy said. She disappeared into the other room, still carrying Brenda.

Aunt Rose led Dad to the couch. "Just relax. I'll make some tea." She turned to Ozzy. "Do you drink tea?"

"No, thanks."

"Then I'll make you some soup."

"I'm not hungry," he said, but Aunt Rose didn't pay any attention. As soon as she left, Dad went back to the painting and stood there staring.

"Why?" he said in a strangled voice. "Why, Gwen, why?"

"Dad?"

Dad kept talking in a low, ragged voice. "You do everything the hard way. Why? Why?"

Ozzy moved forward and touched his arm.

"Dad, hey . . ."

Suddenly Dad collapsed on top of Ozzy, wrapping his arms around him and sobbing. It was more unreal than Mom's death, having Dad cry in his arms. Ozzy didn't know what to do. He wanted to say something but he didn't know what, so he just stood there. It seemed like forever until Sissy came back and put her arms around Dad and led him to the couch. Dad brought out his handkerchief and blew his nose. "I'm sorry."

Sissy gave Ozzy a "what happened?" look, and Ozzy just shook his head. She sat down beside Dad and held his hand. After a moment, Dad put away the handkerchief and said, "What about Lance? Did you reach him?"

"He's taking the first flight out."

"When? What time does it arrive?"

"I don't know. He said he'd call from the airport."

Peter arrived as Aunt Rose brought in tea and soup. He wore a dark, three-piece wool suit without an overcoat, and the snow lay melting on his shoulders like tiny jewels. He and Sissy talked a minute in the hall before coming into the living room. Peter put a hand on Dad's shoulder.

"Frank, I don't know what to say." Then he turned to Ozzy. "I'm sorry, Oz."

Ozzy half-shrugged. Peter was a nice guy, but his manner seemed a little too perfect, like he was in a very sad courtroom. The whole night was like that. Everything seemed a little too much one way or the other. Everything was out of joint.

"Is it too hot?" Aunt Rose asked.

"What?"

"The soup? Is it too hot?"

"No, it's fine," Ozzy said automatically. He stirred the soup without looking at it.

Peter started asking questions, and Dad explained what had happened. The road had been narrow and rutted, with edges walled with packed snow. After parking, they'd hiked until they found the right tree. It only took a few minutes to cut it down, but rather than drag it uphill, they decided to slide it down until they reached another part of the road. Mom went to get the car, and when she didn't show up, Dad went to look for her. It was a one-lane road with turnouts every now and then where you could turn around, but Mom hadn't done that. She put the Bronco into four-wheel drive and pulled onto the snow-covered shoulder. The ledge had given way, and the car had tumbled over the cliff.

"She looked normal," Dad said in a low voice. "Like she was sleeping. So I just thought . . . at first I thought she was unconscious. But then I touched her . . ."

Dad's lips trembled, his face was ashen. Ozzy looked away, but the words continued. Mom's neck had been broken. She hadn't been wearing a seatbelt and was thrown against the roof.

Ozzy felt a sick surge of anger. Why did it have to be Mom? Why was she punished for something as stupid as seatbelts? He remembered the arguments she had had with Dad. "I won't go through life afraid," she would say, and Dad would say, "When I'm driving, everyone wears seatbelts." Only this time Dad hadn't been there to argue with her. Nobody had been there.

Ozzy stood up. "Excuse me."

Dad looked over. "Where are you going?"

"Up to my room."

"Ozzy?"

He kept going and was halfway up the stairs when Peter came into the hallway and called after him. "Hey, buddy, are you all right?"

"I'm fine."

"You're sure?"

Ozzy turned and looked down at him. Peter stood with one hand on the bannister, his eyes clouded with concern.

"I just want to be alone."

He went upstairs to the bathroom, shut the door, and turned on the water. He rested his forehead on his wrists and let the water wash over his hands while he fought the sick feeling in his stomach. He stood that way, breathing deeply, until he felt better. Then he went into the bedroom, lay down, and stared at the ceiling. There were the same designs in the plaster that had always been there—the surprised camel, the dog with two tails, the bear with sideways eyes, the silly groundhog Mom had discovered, lying there with him one day, helping him find ceiling animals.

"Mom, Mom, Mom, Mom," he found himself whispering. It was hard to believe that the mountains had killed her. Mom loved the mountains. Every summer she made Dad drop her off in one of the canyons and she'd disappear for three days. "My retreat," she called it. She took a sleeping bag and a backpack, and on the third day at six o'clock she'd show up at the same spot to be picked up. Dad worried each day she was gone but he couldn't talk her out of doing it.

"I don't understand what you do up there."

"I walk and stand still, mostly."

"I don't understand why I can't come with you."

"You might move while I'm standing still."

The mountains were like an old friend to Mom; they would never kill her. Besides, Mom was too strong, too vital, too wrapped up in life for some stupid accident to tear her away. If she were dead, he would feel it. Things would be different. The sun would be a different shape, the air would smell like sulfur, a hot wind would parch the mountains and grind them into desert, the ceiling animals would disappear . . .

His mind went around in circles chasing and being chased by a dark cloud with no shape and no definition and no beginning and no end, a void of pain just out of reach, waiting to suck him in. Finally he fell into a fitful sleep and began to dream.

In the dream they were standing on a rocky peak up near the Continental Divide, everybody except Mom. It was barely dawn and the first rays of the sun came sweeping across the Kansas plains. Ozzy knew why they were there. Mom had said she wanted to be cremated, and now, as he watched, Dad passed his hand in an arc, and Mom's ashes leaped into the wind. The ashes formed an image—an image of Mom, touched by the sun, shifting, dancing, glowing in the early morning light—and in that moment, Mom gave a secret smile and pointed to him in the way that meant she was counting on him to do something special for her, but Ozzy didn't know what it was. He tried to ask her but he couldn't speak, and then Dad and the others turned toward him, and Ozzy knew he was supposed to do something, and he turned toward Mom to ask, "What?" but a gust of wind came and her image dissolved . . .

He woke up. It was dark, and something was touching his face, tiny pinpricks on his cheeks and forehead. It took a second before he realized they were snowflakes. The window was open, and snow was drifting into the room. He sat up, and something next to the bed moved.

"Ozzy?"

He jerked back and banged his head against the wall.

"Take it easy," the voice said.

"Lance?"

"Yeah." A lumpy shadow moved across the room, patting the wall. "Where's the light switch?"

Ozzy rolled to one side and turned on the lamp beside the bed.

"Ah!" Lance squinted and held his hand against the light. He was wearing a ratty pea coat and a purple knit cap. Long black hair flowed out from the cap and became a beard as it passed his ears.

"Lance! What are you—"

The memory of Mom's death knocked the words back into his throat. He'd forgotten. Lance noticed his expression.

"What's wrong?"

"I just remembered."

Lance stood there with a somber expression, chunks of snow melting to the floor. "Shit, Ozzy," he said softly. He bit his lip, stepped forward, and gave Ozzy a big hug. Mom's death had brought Lance home, and for a moment Ozzy remembered the way it had been, growing up with this big athletic guy who was his brother, Lance, with a gorgeous smile and infectious laugh, Lance, the guy everybody loved.

"Now she belongs to the ages," Lance whispered. "Time and tides come full circle."

A cold wind blew through the room. Ozzy got up and

closed the window. Outside on the roof Lance's footprints were visible in the snow.

"Why didn't you ring the doorbell?"

"Didn't need to."

"But how'd you get on the roof?"

"Climbed the clothesline pole. Didn't I ever show you that trick?"

"No."

"I used to climb the roof every time I stayed out all night and didn't want to argue with the folks." He took off his coat and tossed it in the corner. "You got a towel or something?"

"You want to take a bath?"

Lance patted his head. "My hair. I feel like a sponge."

The towels were in a closet down the hall, but Ozzy was afraid he might wake somebody, so he got an old sweatshirt out of the dresser and gave it to Lance.

"I don't believe how fast you got here."

"Tell me about it." His words were muffled as he ran the sweatshirt over his beard. "I didn't know if I'd get through immigration. Figured if I was on the list, they'd haul my ass back to jail."

"What list?"

"The pickup list. I broke parole when I went to Canada. That's why I used this." Lance pulled out a worn wallet and handed it to Ozzy. "The Jeff Waxman driver's license. Check out the expiration date."

Inside the wallet was a California driver's license with Lance's picture and the name Jeff Waxman.

"What is this? This isn't you."

A big smile appeared in Lance's beard. "It's the

handy-dandy Jeff Waxman universal driver's license. We all use it, only somebody forgot to keep it up-to-date. Check out the expiration date. I didn't even realize it until the dude at Immigration said, 'Don't you drive anymore?' I didn't know what he was talking about until he showed me the expiration date."

"Who's Jeff Waxman?"

"He's nobody. Just a name some of us use when we come to the States. There are a lot of us who don't feel comfortable down here, who don't want our movements traced, our histories put down in punch cards, our files updated and records checked. The eagle doesn't see any borders, the deer don't go through Immigration, trout don't fill out customs declarations, why should we? We let Jeff Waxman do it for us."

Ozzy was still thinking of what Lance had said earlier. "I didn't know you broke parole."

"Neither do the folks, so keep it to yourself." Lance sat down. "Dad, I mean."

For a moment they were both silent, both thinking the same thing. There was only Dad now. Then Ozzy said, "How come you did all that stuff, Lance? Dealing drugs and everything?" Lance looked up slowly. "I mean, if you don't want to talk about it . . ."

"Why not? It's all ancient history now."

He slumped back in the chair and used both hands to push the hair back from his forehead. Ozzy was surprised to see he had a receding hairline.

"I don't know," he said. "I went to Stanford, thought I was going to breeze through the place. Thought I'd be on the team, quarterback, halfback anyway, same as I was here. Big hero, you know. Mom was going to fly out when we reached the play-offs. What a joke. I didn't even make second string."

"I know. You wouldn't brown-nose the coach."

"What?"

"You know—the team politics."

"Where'd you hear that?"

"I remember when Mom went out there."

"Oh, yeah. Well, after she reamed the coach, I was never going to get on the team."

"What do you mean?"

"She came out there like a mother hen, ready to scratch his eyes out. Told the coach he was too antagonistic."

"She did?"

"I didn't even know she was there. She watched us practice and took the coach aside and told him he'd never seen my full potential because the environment was wrong. What a joke."

"Maybe it was."

"Oz, I was lousy. That's why I didn't make the team."

"That's not what Mom said."

"Mom? She didn't know. She had no idea."

Ozzy felt himself stiffen. It didn't seem right for Lance to be criticizing Mom. Not the way she always tried to support him and the way he'd let her down.

"So why'd you smuggle drugs?"

"Success, what else? I wasn't making it on the gridiron, wasn't making it in the classroom, so I was going to make it as a dope smuggler. I had it all planned—I was going to come back here driving a Porsche, take the folks to Europe, buy you and Sissy a bunch of new clothes, all that materialistic bullshit."

"You were going to buy me new clothes?"

"Clothes, new stereo, anything you wanted, anything anybody wanted." Lance made a face. "It's all coming back to me, how bad I wanted to be a success."

"You could have been. You really could."

"Not that way."

"Mom always said you could have been anything you wanted."

Lance looked at him with a strange expression. "I am, Oz. I am what I want to be."

Looking at the big, bearded guy sitting in front of him with matted hair and smelly, rain-soaked clothes, all Ozzy could think was, Then you don't want to be much.

Lance started unlacing his boots. "So how'd it happen? Sissy didn't say much on the phone."

Ozzy told him how Mom was trying to turn around when part of the road gave way. Lance shook his head. "That's just like her, huh? Always looking for a shortcut."

"It wasn't her, Lance. It was the road."

"Whatever." Lance chucked his boots in a corner. "You got some smoke?"

"What?"

"Got some grass? A spare joint maybe?"

Ozzy shook his head. He had a low tolerance for drugs of any kind. Just taking aspirin made him feel like he could walk through walls, and the one time he'd gotten stoned, he spent the night hiding under the bed fighting panic and listening to the clock tick.

"I got to score something," Lance said. "I'm not going to make it through the funeral unless I take the edge off."

"It won't be a funeral exactly. Mom wanted to be cremated and have just the family around."

Lance raised his arms to stretch and caught a whiff of his armpit. He wrinkled his nose. "I think I need a bath."

Ozzy got two towels, figuring Lance would need one for the beard alone. As he stepped past him into the hallway , Lance whispered, "Talk about déjà vu. I never thought I'd see this place again."

Outside the bedroom window it was growing light. The snow had stopped, but the sky was still overcast and the world seemed somber and gray. Only the streetlights seemed alive, floating in the gloom like miniature yellow spaceships. Ozzy went to the dresser and took down one of the photos stuck along the edge of the frame holding the mirror. It was a picture of Mom and Dad, taken last summer on their trip to Vancouver. They were standing on a ferryboat to Victoria with a lot of Japanese tourists near them. It was weird to think that the tourists were still alive back home in Japan, while Mom was dead.

He sat down, holding the picture like a precious jewel. It was easier to believe that Mom was on that ferryboat or off on one of her European tours than to think she was gone forever. She had been away from home before, sometimes for a couple of weeks, and it was no different today than if she were on a trip. It was no different as long as he didn't think too far into the future. It was the future that hurt, the forever without her.

Someone screamed. Ozzy jumped up and ran into the hallway. Aunt Rose stood clutching her robe, her back against the wall, staring at the bathroom door.

"Oh my God, oh my God—"

Sissy's door flew open, and Peter came out in dark blue bikini underwear, with Sissy in a robe right behind. "What is it?"

"Aunt Rose?"

Dad appeared in faded-yellow pajamas. "Who screamed?"

"In the tub," Aunt Rose gasped.

From behind the bathroom door came Lance's voice, "Relax, relax, we've all got bodies . . ." A moment later he appeared with a towel around his waist, hair dripping like a wet poodle. "Hi, everybody."

Sissy recognized him first. "Lance!" she screamed. She ran forward and threw her arms around him.

"He got here a little while ago," Ozzy said, "and nobody was up so . . ."

Aunt Rose put a palm to her forehead. "He scared me to death."

It must have been the way she said it, because Peter stuck his hand in front of his mouth to keep from laughing, and Dad couldn't help smiling. Then everybody was laughing, everybody but Aunt Rose, all at once. It was crazy laughter, and it stopped almost as soon as it started. Everybody felt a little guilty, but they all felt better, too. With Lance back, it was like being a whole family again.

The feeling lasted about two hours, until Ozzy found out what kind of funeral service they planned. Then the whole world fell apart.

Chapter 6

AT FIRST it seemed like Aunt Rose's fault and later Sissy's fault, but really the problem was Dad giving in to everybody. The first clue Ozzy had was before breakfast, when he was helping Aunt Rose. She was making a big deal out of having the family together again, so she wanted to use the dining room table and get out the best silver and china. Ozzy got stuck polishing napkin holders while Dad took a shower and Peter and Brenda drove to the store to get English muffins and Grape Nuts Flakes. Sissy and Lance huddled in the living room talking a mile a minute about people they had known in high school.

"Here." Aunt Rose handed him a candelabra that they never used. "We'll need this for the reception."

"What reception?"

"After the funeral." She disappeared into the kitchen. Ozzy paused a moment, and the polish dried in white streaks around his fingers. Aunt Rose wasn't really part of the family and didn't understand about the small, intimate service Mom wanted. A few minutes later, Sissy called him into the living room and shut the door quietly. Lance was sitting on the couch.

"Ozzy," Sissy said with a delicate frown, "why did you tell Lance that Mother was being cremated?"

Ozzy stared at her. The dream last night was so real, it was as if they were talking about something that had already happened.

"What do you mean?"

"I mean you told Lance that Mother was being cremated, didn't you?"

"Sure, because that's what she wanted."

"That's not true, Ozzy. Mother is having a Christian funeral and is going to be buried in the family plot."

"What family plot?"

"Grandma arranged for a family plot at Saint Boniface in Denver. Mother's going to be buried beside her. We discussed all this last night while you were asleep." She made it sound like he was a criminal for sleeping.

"I was awake a long time."

"Fine, but just so you realize, the wake is Tuesday and the funeral is Wednesday morning."

"A wake?"

"Of course a wake." Sissy reached for her purse and got out a pack of cigarettes. "Mother was a Catholic."

Ozzy was stunned. Mom might have been born a Catholic, but she was never a practicing one. In fact, she hated organized religion of any kind. "More people have killed each other for somebody's god than for any other reason," she used to say. Mom hadn't made made a sincere cross sign in ages, and the idea of her being laid out and stared at and prayed over was embarrassing. It was like watching her when she was going to the bathroom or something.

"Break off the filter," Lance said. He was talking to Sissy. She had the cigarette between her lips and was looking for her lighter. "What?"

"The filter. Break it off. It'll help you cut down."

"I don't want to cut down." Sissy found the lighter and took short, decisive puffs as she lit the cigarette. A sense of panic began to take hold of Ozzy. He tried to keep his voice calm.

"Sissy, Mom wanted to be cremated, don't you remember? She always said we should take her ashes to the Continental Divide at dawn."

"Oh, Ozzy." She waved his words away. "She was just joking."

"No, she wasn't. She was serious."

Sissy's smile became tight, and her eyes narrowed in a way that he remembered from when they were kids. "Really? Then what about the white horses? Do you think she was serious about *them,* too?"

"That part doesn't matter."

"Why not? If she was serious about the cremation, she must have been serious about the white horses."

"What white horses?" Lance wanted to know.

Sissy turned to him. "He's talking about this silly thing Mom said about scattering her ashes from white horses at dawn."

"It wasn't silly."

"White horses?" Lance smiled. "Yeah, that sounds like her."

"She wasn't serious," Sissy said.

Ozzy could feel the ceremony slipping away, the ceremony Mom would have wanted. He turned to Lance. "What do you think? Doesn't it sound more like Mom to have a private ceremony with just the family?"

Sissy whipped the cigarette from her mouth and spit the smoke away. "It doesn't matter what anybody thinks. The Church doesn't sanction cremation, and Father wants a Christian burial and Aunt Rose offered the family plot, so let's just stop talking about it, all right?"

She stared right at Ozzy, and for a moment there was this dead silence. Trying to look at Sissy when she was mad was like trying to stare at the sun. Ozzy looked away and said in a low voice, "Grandpa didn't have a Catholic funeral."

"He wasn't a Catholic."

"Well, all I'm saying is what Mom said."

"She said white horses, Ozzy! Do you honestly think we're supposed to rent dozens of white horses and get trucks to haul them to the Continental Divide? And drivers to drive the trucks and wranglers to saddle the horses and everybody getting up at four A.M. to be there at dawn? I mean, does all that sound serious?"

Ozzy was ready to tell her what she could do with her never-ending white horses, but he knew that it was useless to argue with Sissy. Once she reached a certain point, it was like an atom bomb reaching critical mass, and nothing would stop it from blowing up.

The door burst open, and Brenda came running in with a bouquet of sweetheart roses.

"Mommy, guess what? Daddy let me buy flowers for Grandma."

"They're very pretty, honey. Why don't you ask Aunt Rose to put them in water?"

"Wait a minute." Lance knelt down. "Can I smell them first?"

Brenda hesitated. Lance was wearing clean army fatigues, but he still looked like a Rasputin mountain man. "C'mon." Lance lifted his nose and sniffed the air. "Let me smell."

Brenda inched forward like she was feeding hay to a horse, and Lance made a big deal over smelling the flowers. Sissy took a deep breath and let it out slowly.

"Let's not argue," she said softly. "Dad's made his decision, and the rest of us agree with him, so please don't go upsetting everybody by arguing about it, okay?" She gave him a forgiving smile.

Peter came to the door and held up a prescription drug container. "Do you want these now or with breakfast?"

"I need one now." Sissy took Brenda's hand. "Come on, honey, let's get some nice water for your flowers."

They disappeared into the kitchen, and Lance said, "Sweet kid." Ozzy was still shaken, half by the argument and half by what they planned to do to Mom.

"What do you think?" he asked. "I mean about what Mom wanted?"

Lance made a gesture to take in the room. "This is civilization, Oz, what do you expect? Nobody's in tune with the natural order."

"Mom was."

"She was in tune with herself."

"But it's what she wanted, I know it."

"That's what her consciousness wanted, not her essence." He put an arm around Ozzy's shoulder. "The consciousness dies with the body, but the essence lives in here." He tapped Ozzy's chest. "You listen to Mom's essence and you find out something. You know what you find out? She doesn't give a shit! I flashed on that while you and Sissy were talking. If there's anybody in the world who didn't care what happened to her body, it was Mom. Know what I mean?"

"I don't know . . ."

"Let the body worshipers do what they want," he whispered. "They can't touch her. Like the song says, she's far beyond the pale."

Lance's half-baked philosophy was almost as bad as Sissy's steel-edged anger. None of it made him feel any better. It was then that he realized it wasn't up to Sissy or Lance what happened with Mom. It was up to Dad. Ozzy felt a surge of hope. Neither Sissy nor Lance had been around Mom for years. How could they know what she wanted? But Dad had been there, just like him. He knew her, and he knew the kind of ceremony she wanted. Dad wouldn't let them screw up Mom's memory with a gross public ceremony, he was sure of it. Dad wasn't even a Catholic. All Ozzy had to do was get him alone and talk to him, using the same rapport from when Dad cried on his shoulder yesterday. As soon as he thought of it, he wanted to go upstairs and find Dad, but breakfast was ready, so he had to wait.

Breakfast was weird without Mom. It was weird because everybody's place was changed. Lance was in Mom's chair, just to the right of Dad. Ozzy was usually on Dad's left, but now Sissy was there, so that Brenda could sit between her and Peter. Instead, Ozzy sat opposite Brenda between Lance and Aunt Rose. It didn't feel right.

As soon as everybody was seated, Dad banged his spoon against his coffee cup and called for quiet.

"I, uh, I think we should make a toast." He lifted up his orange juice glass and spoke in a hesitant voice that went up and down like a warped record. "I just want to say that, uh, we welcome Lance back home and . . . I don't think anything would have made Mom happier than to know the family is back together again. I think she knows that."

They all lifted their glasses and drank orange juice, pretending not to be embarrassed. It was Dad's way of trying to strike an optimistic note, which he tended to do no matter what.

Nobody was all that hungry, but Aunt Rose had the table loaded with bran muffins, grapefruit, cereal, orange juice, poached eggs, and sausage. They didn't talk about Mom, but there was a layer of sadness below everything that was said, and every once in a while somebody would stop eating and get this empty look in his eyes and you knew he was thinking about her. Ozzy was waiting for breakfast to end so that he could talk to Dad about having the mountain ceremony. The more he thought about it, the more angry he got with Sissy. The reason she wanted a big church service was because she was a born-again Catholic. She had become a big convert the year after Lance was arrested, when Mom and Dad were unhappy and argued a lot. Sissy made friends with an Italian girl, Brenda Delgado, who put her in touch with her Catholic roots. Brenda Delgado was maid of honor at Sissy's wedding and was little Brenda's namesake. She was a fierce Catholic and turned Sissy into one, but neither of them could get Mom to return to the fold.

"The monks censored Sappho," Mom said. She told this story of how the Catholic monks were in charge of translating Greek poetry during the Dark Ages, and since they hated female homosexuality, they threw away most of Sappho's poetry. "I see more of God's footprints in the snow," Mom always said, "than in all the churches of the world."

Not Sissy, though. Sissy and Brenda Delgado saw God's footprints all over the church. They even tried to get Ozzy into the fold. They took him to some introductory masses and had him interview with a nun, but the whole thing seemed too sloppy and inefficient. You had to spend all your time worshiping the mother of the son of the God who you want to worship in the first place. Ozzy could never figure out why Jesus' mother was so important. She probably didn't even have to be human, since the whole thing was a miracle to begin with. It would have saved a lot of arguments if Jesus had been born of a goat or a squirrel instead of a woman. There would have been no doubt that he was the son of God and you wouldn't need Crusades or Inquisitions to try and prove it. Best of all would be to skip Jesus and have God show up on your eighteenth birthday, do a miracle to prove who he was, and then tell you exactly what he wanted you to do for the rest of your life. That would be the most efficient system of all, and nobody would dare argue about it.

All during breakfast the doorbell kept ringing with flowers being delivered. Aunt Rose wrote down who sent what kind of flowers and when they arrived. She was very organized when it came to the death business, maybe because her husband had died. Later when Dad was sipping coffee she said, "I told the funeral home we'd be there at eleven. Is that all right?"

Dad just nodded and kept rocking the coffee cup between his hands as if he was trying to warm them up. Ozzy almost said something right then, but Sissy was watching him like a hawk. Dad kept silent while Aunt Rose suggested a few other things, like whether to have candles at the wake and what kind of announcements to send out. Finally he left the table and went upstairs to get dressed. Ozzy tried to be clever about it. He started clearing the table, and when Sissy wasn't looking, he slipped upstairs.

"Hey, Dad?"

The door was open, so he walked right in. Dad was standing at his dresser. He had a tie draped over his collar, but his hands were still. He was staring into the mirror like a man looking at a cobra. It was one of those private looks you're not supposed to see, but the other person knows you did, so you both pretend like nobody saw anything. Dad concentrated on his tie.

"Are they ready?"

"No. Still clearing the table."

"Oh, good."

"I was helping them."

"That's great."

It was a dumb conversation, but it took Ozzy a minute to recover from seeing the terrible look on Dad's face.

"That Aunt Rose is a good cook," Dad said.

Ozzy sat down on the bed. He had to get things back to the father-son rapport they had had last night.

"It's just like the old days, huh, Dad? Now that Lance is back?"

Dad nodded. "I'm glad he came back."

"Yeah, so am I. It makes me remember the old days, you know? The whole family, everybody together. I remember it very clearly."

Dad was fumbling with his tie. He wasn't doing so hot. The phone rang downstairs, and Ozzy knew he didn't have much time.

"Say, Dad, there's something I wanted to check with you. It's about this funeral idea, you know? I mean, I know it's nice and everything, but aren't we going to do it the way Mom said? Up in the mountains with the family?"

"In the mountains?"

"You know, like when she said in case something ever happened, we should hold a farewell ceremony in the mountains at dawn. Remember?" He felt like he had marbles in his mouth. In the mirror Dad looked confused.

"You want to bury Mother in the mountains?"

"Not bury her. Her remains. You know, her ashes. Cast her ashes into the wind at dawn, just like she said."

Dad's eyes shifted back to his tie. "Well, Ozzy, I, uh, I think the funeral arrangements have already been made."

"Who made the arrangements?"

"Well, we're going down this morning to sign the papers."

"But you don't have to sign them."

Dad kept his eyes on his hands as he adjusted his collar.

"Dad?"

"Ummm?"

"You don't have to sign the papers, do you? I mean, you could sign the papers for taking her ashes to the mountains instead of a burial, right?"

"I think Aunt Rose has already arranged for Mother to be buried beside your grandmother. We have a family plot, did you know that?"

"But Mom didn't want a family plot." He could hear the desperate edge in his voice, but he couldn't help it. "She wanted a ceremony in the mountains."

"The Rubicoffs just called and—" Sissy came into the room and saw Ozzy. She paused and then continued more slowly. "—they wanted to make a donation in Mother's name. They wanted to know if you had a favorite charity."

"That's fine." Dad sounded relieved. Sissy cocked her head at Ozzy. "You're coming with us, aren't you?"

"I don't know." He looked at her and she looked at him. They were each waiting for the other one to leave. Finally Sissy said, "Well, if you are, you'd better go get ready. We have to go soon."

"I want to talk to Dad first."

Sissy's smile grew thin. "What about?"

"Something private."

"Ozzy . . ." She made his name into a warning. "I asked you not to upset anybody."

"Now, now." Dad stepped forward. "We were just

talking about the best kind of service to hold, that's all."

Sissy kept her eyes on Ozzy. "We settled this before breakfast. I don't understand why—"

"We didn't settle anything." He was angry now. "You're not doing what she wanted."

"How do you know what she wanted, Ozzy? She didn't leave a will. What gives you the right to decide what she wanted?"

"She told me. She told all of us."

"All right," Dad said. "That's enough."

Ozzy turned to him. "Tell her. You know what she said."

"Leave him alone, Ozzy."

"Just let him answer."

"He doesn't have to answer; we know what Mom wanted."

"*You* don't. You don't even live here."

"She was my mother, too, don't forget."

"Easy, easy," Dad said, but it was too late. They were yelling now.

"Then you didn't know her very well," Ozzy said, "or you'd know she didn't want any big church funeral."

"I knew her better than you did, but you don't care about that. All you care about is getting things done your way. Little Ozzy Mills has to decide everything—"

Ozzy could see her mouth moving, sharp and tight like a machine snapping back and forth, changing everything around so instead of her jamming everything down everybody's throat, it was him.

"You should talk," he yelled. "You're 'the Little D,' Sissy, that's what she called you—the little disappointment. That's how well you know her."

Dad's voice was suddenly firm. "That's enough, Ozzy."

"It's true! Tell her."

"It's not true."

"It is so!"

Dad grabbed him. "Will you shut up?"

Suddenly they were like strangers, like enemies, Sissy with her stricken look, Dad desperately clutching his arm. He wrenched free.

"It's your fault," he yelled at Dad. "Why'd you let her drive? Why? Why?"

And then he was running, out of the house and into the street, faster and faster until his feet were numb and his throat was raw and the hot tears grew cold and froze upon his cheeks.

Chapter 7

HE HAD LEFT THE HOUSE without a jacket, and it was a lot colder today than yesterday. Ozzy was freezing in his black shirt and pants. To get warm, he ducked into a 7-Eleven, where there were a bunch of sixth-graders playing video games and yelling, "Go for it! Go for it!" Ozzy wandered aimlessly up and down the aisles while he calmed down. The shock on Dad's face was still vivid in his memory, but every time he started to feel bad about it, he thought of how Dad had known what a lousy driver Mom was. He knew she was always getting into trouble speeding and taking shortcuts through alleys and parking lots and making U-turns in the middle of the street. He should never have let her drive in the mountains.

"Hey, kid," the guy at the cash register called. "You looking for something?" Ozzy pretended not to hear.

"Hey, you." This time the guy yelled it real loud, and all the sixth-graders turned to look. Ozzy picked up a can of dog food and turned around. "Are you talking to me?"

"What do you need?" the guy said, more friendly now that Ozzy had some merchandise in his hand. He was a skinny guy, with stringy hair combed from one ear up over his bald spot.

"Just this." Ozzy went to the counter, put the dog food on it, and kept walking, right out the door.

"Wise guy," the clerk called. "Come in here again and I'll—"

The door closed, and Ozzy started jogging. By the time he felt safe enough to slow down, he was grinning. For some reason, doing something totally juvenile always cheered him up. But he still didn't want to go home. He couldn't face Dad until he knew what he was going to do. In the dream Mom had pointed to him as if she were giving him a mission; now he knew what it was. He was the one who had to keep Mom's memory alive the way she was, not the way everybody tried to pretend she was. Mom was special and she wanted a special kind of funeral. It was up to Ozzy to fulfill her last wishes.

The only place he could go was Gary's house. As usual, it took ten minutes of pounding on the biology-lab door to pull Gary away from his experiments.

"Ozzy?" Gary stood blinking in the doorway. "What are you doing here?"

"Freezing to death. You want to let me in, or what?"

Gary jumped back, and Ozzy went to the heating duct in the floor and stood on top of it so that the warm air drifted up his pant legs.

Gary said, "Don't you have a coat?"

"I forgot it. I had this blowup with Dad and everybody. All about Mom."

He didn't know if Gary had heard, but as soon as he mentioned Mom's name, Gary's expression changed.

"Ozzy, I'm really sorry. I called last night, but they said you were asleep. Are you okay?"

"You called last night?"

"As soon as I heard what happened. Didn't you get my message?"

"No way. Nobody tells me anything." Ozzy pulled his shirt out and let the heat come up across his chest. Gary stood in the middle of the room, shifting his weight uneasily and looking as if he wanted to say something but was afraid to.

"What?" Ozzy demanded.

"We heard . . . was it really an avalanche?"

"An avalanche?"

"You know—that knocked the car off the road?"

"Where'd you hear that?"

"An engineer who works with Dad called last night. He heard it somewhere."

"It was an accident, Gary. The car went over a cliff."

"How'd it happen? I mean, if you want to talk about it."

Ozzy explained what had happened and was surprised that it wasn't as hard telling Gary as it had been telling Lance. Getting angry with Dad and Sissy made it easier to talk about Mom. When he was finished, Gary said, "You mean nobody heard it happen?"

"No, I told you."

"Was it windy?"

"How should I know? I wasn't there."

Gary chewed his lip, lost in thought. "Maybe the temperature was abnormally cold."

"What difference does that make?"

"Well, sound waves are influenced by temperature. If the ambient air temperature was extra low, it might have inhibited the sound of the car starting."

"Oh, that's really important, Gary. Maybe you can figure out why nobody heard her *scream* as she went over the edge."

"Oh no, Ozzy." Gary's features started jerking around. "I wasn't trying to—I mean, there's no disrespect or anything. I like your mom. I mean, liked her. I'm not making fun, you know that, don't you?"

Instead of answering, Ozzy went to stand in front of the worm tanks. He hated how living people changed dead people around. Mom was already becoming unreal. Sissy wanted to make her an ideal Catholic, Aunt Rose thought it was a big social occasion, Dad didn't know what to think, and Gary treated it like a science project. Mom was getting lost, he could feel it.

"So what was the blowup?"

"What?"

"With your dad. You said—"

"Oh, that." Ozzy sat down on a stool next to a metal table. He leaned forward, but the table was cold on his forearms, so he sat straight and folded his arms. "Let me ask you a question, as a neutral observer. What would you do if your mom died and she wanted to be buried one way and the family wanted to bury her another way?"

Gary looked confused. "You mean like standing up?"

"No, stupid, that's just an example—"

"All right, all right."

"—a hypothetical, like you use in all these science projects, you know?"

"I said all right."

The quick flash of anger died and left Ozzy puzzled. Why was he so upset with Gary? The guy didn't even know what was going on. He took a deep breath and started from the beginning, explaining how Mom had wanted a ceremony in the mountains and Sissy had derailed the whole thing into a big church ceremony. When he was finished, Gary shook his head and said, "God, she sounds tough."

"Who, Sissy?"

"I always wished I had brothers and sisters, but when I hear something like that, it makes me glad I don't."

"It's not her that pisses me off as much as Dad. It's his fault."

"Because he agrees with her?"

Because he let her drive the car, Ozzy wanted to say. But he couldn't tell Gary that. Gary wasn't part of the family, and it would be like betraying Dad the same way Dad was betraying Mom. If only he were famous, people would listen to him. They'd do anything he wanted. He remembered seeing this classic movie, *Citizen Kane.* It was all about the richest man in the world, who collected childhood sleds and could do anything he wanted. Charles Foster Kane, that was his name . . .

Ozzy imagined them at the graveyard, Dad and everybody beside tombstones and tons of people and a priest ready to give Mom a fancy funeral and lower the casket into the ground when this three-mile-long limousine arrives. The crowd parts like the Red Sea and the limousine pulls up right in front of the grave. The roof slides back, and a pedestal rises with the richest man in the world on it. He wears a black suit worth fifty thousand dollars and he leans into the wind and raises an arm high above his head. "I AM CHARLES FOSTER KANE AND YOU WILL NOT BURY MY MOTHER!"

"Ozzy?"

"What?"

Gary was watching him with a worried expression. "Are you okay?"

"Yeah, sure." He got up from the stool. "I just wish—"

He stopped as an idea struck. You only needed to be a millionaire if you wanted to stop a funeral in public, right out where everybody could see it. But there were other ways of doing it, more devious ways. He turned to Gary.

"How much money have you got?"

"Money?"

"In cash. Right now, in the house."

"In my room I've got, I don't know, maybe twenty bucks."

"That's all?" He was disappointed. He figured that since Gary was from a rich family, he'd have lots of cash lying around.

"Why? What do you need?"

"A hundred and fifty-six dollars, that's how much is in my bank account. What about your dad? Could he loan me that much?"

"What for?"

"Better you don't know. Just go ask him, okay?"

Gary looked uncomfortable. "What am I supposed to tell him I want it for?"

"Won't he just loan it to you?"

"A hundred and fifty-six dollars?"

"Tell him anything. Tell him you're going to buy a new microscope or new worms or something."

"Oh sure."

Ozzy grabbed his arm and pushed him to the door. "Gary, will you just do me this favor, please? Just get him to give you the money."

"How am I supposed to pay him back?"

"I'll write you a check. Look." Ozzy whipped out his wallet and unfolded a wrinkled blank check. "See?"

"If you're going to do that, why don't I give you the money? I can go to the bank."

"Because it's Sunday, in case you forgot."

"That doesn't matter. First National has an automatic teller. I can get money anytime."

He should have known. Rich people might not carry cash, but they carried lots of cards that could make cash appear at a moment's notice.

Gary loaned him a ski parka that was about sixteen sizes too big and sat on his back like a red igloo. They drove to the bank on Gary's moped. The automatic teller gave out only even amounts of money, so Ozzy made out a check for one hundred and fifty dollars. When they were done, he had Gary drop him at the Laundromat on the corner of Sixth and Elm.

"Why here?" Gary asked.

Ozzy pulled up the oversize collar of the jacket and spoke out of the side of his mouth like a gangster. "Listen, you don't ask no questions, see? What you don't know won't hurt you."

But he couldn't kid Gary out of being worried. "Just promise me—you're not planning on . . . hurting yourself or anything?"

Ozzy laughed. For a guy who didn't watch any TV, Gary had a real soap-opera view of the world. What did he think he was going to do? Tumble himself to death in a clothes dryer?

"I'm going to fix things, Gary, that's all. Don't worry."

He waited until Gary disappeared around the corner, then walked three blocks up Elm until he could see Lacey's Funeral Home. Aunt Rose's Lincoln was parked out front, so he knew they were still there. He moved behind a tree, stuck his hands into the jacket pockets to keep them warm, and waited. In the west, the clouds were beginning to break, and a shaft of sunlight spilled over white mountain peaks. It was a good sign. Ozzy fingered the wad of bills. He hoped Old Man Lacey was greedy. He hoped he was the greediest man in the world.

Chapter 8

LACEY'S FUNERAL HOME was a two-storied house that had been turned into a mortuary but was still supposed to look like a house. Actually the Laceys did live there, in the upstairs part. Downstairs was reserved for the death business. As soon as Dad and everybody left, Ozzy went up the circular driveway to the office. There was a sign on the door: Welcome. Please Step Inside. He hesitated. Now that it was time to do it—to actually bribe Old Man Lacey—he felt uneasy. He didn't feel like Charles Foster Kane. He felt like a scared kid who was going to do something dipshit.

"Grace under pressure." Ernest Hemingway's motto came back to him from *Famous Authorship.* Hemingway would never feel like a baby in front of an undertaker. He had been shot at by real bullets and gored by real bulls. The problem with America was that it didn't offer good manhood experiences anymore. Ozzy didn't have that much experience facing fear and being courageous. He thought about Mom and remembered that this was the last thing he could ever do for her. He took a deep breath and pushed open the door.

There was the smell of roast pork coming from upstairs and the sound of clinking silverware and people talking. When the door opened, far-off chimes played the first seven notes of "Rock of Ages" and things grew quiet upstairs. It was the Laceys' early-warning system, alerting them to get somber. Old Man Lacey came downstairs, buttoning his coat. He was on the fat side, with pudgy hands and bulldog cheeks, but he had a sympathetic voice that was soft and low and rumbled like Wyoming thunder.

"Come in, come in," Mr. Lacey said. "I'm Howard Lacey."

"I know, Mr. Lacey. I'm Ozzy Mills."

Old Man Lacey snapped his fingers. "Of course. I'm sorry, Ozzy; the last time I saw you was, well . . ." He shook his head, and then his expression changed. "Let me tell you how sorry I was at the news of your mother's passing. She was a fine lady. I offer my condolences."

"Yes, sir."

"If you're looking for your family, they just left not more than two minutes ago."

"I know."

"Even your brother was here, and I didn't even recognize him. Of course it's no wonder, with that beard he's got and me not having seen him since he and Ricky were in high school together. But as I say, you just missed them, just missed them."

Ozzy was nervous. He barely knew Mr. Lacey and he had never bribed anyone before. He had to figure Mr.

Lacey's motivations, like famous authors did when they wrote about people. He pretended that the heavy man with baggy eyes who stood before him with his fingertips touching was a character in a novel. He squinted, and Mr. Lacey became a dark blur. Somewhere there was a secret motivation Ozzy had to find.

"Something wrong, Ozzy?"

"No, sir."

"If you feel faint, you just say something. Times like this, great emotional distress . . ."

Upstairs there was a sudden burst of television noise and then Mrs. Lacey's voice, "Turn it down; there's customers." The volume decreased, and a door slammed. Mr. Lacey looked a little embarrassed.

"Let me show you the casket your father picked out, Ozzy. And the viewing room, so you'll feel familiar come Tuesday."

"Tuesday?"

"For the wake. Tuesday evening, right?"

Ozzy just nodded, and Mr. Lacey led him into a room that used to be a living room and was now a viewing room that was supposed to look like a living room. There were Oriental rugs and lace curtains and a matching velvet couch and chair. Ozzy smiled and nodded at whatever Mr. Lacey said. After the viewing room, they went down the hall to a showroom with half a dozen empty coffins arranged against the wall like giant piano keys. Four were varnished wood, one was pure white, and another ebony black. Mr. Lacey ran his hand down a polished mahogany coffin with brass handles.

"This is the lovely half-couch your father chose. The

bottom half is closed so that we can set a floral arrangement. Your father chose a Robin's Egg design. This one."

Mr. Lacey picked up a fancy three-ring binder with plastic pages and showed him a picture of a fancy arrangement with vines and flowers and powder-blue ribbons and bows.

Ozzy was still trying to figure out his approach. He looked around. "I guess it's more work than you'd think, doing a funeral."

"That's kind of you to say so, Ozzy. Not many people realize the time and attention that goes into finding the proper ceremony for a loved one. But I don't want to burden you with my problems."

"It's no burden," Ozzy said quickly. "It looks like a very interesting business."

Mr. Lacey gave him a look of renewed appreciation. "I'll tell you something, Ozzy. I can't really look at it as a business. My feeling is, being a funeral director isn't a job, it's a calling. That's why I told my sons, 'If it's not in your heart, it's not your part.' And as it turns out, Larry is working for the forest service and Rick is a computer programmer. Neither one of them has it in here." He tapped his chest.

Ozzy felt like he was onto something. Maybe he could appeal to Mr. Lacey's humanitarian instincts.

"It sounds like it takes someone with a special understanding of people."

"That's exactly right, Ozzy. That's why I carry this casket." He walked across the room and whipped a black satin robe off what looked like a packing crate. "A simple Lieber-Helmholtz double-walled pine. Now I know directors who won't carry anything in the basic line, and I have no respect for them. None whatsoever. The director who serves his pocketbook before the public shouldn't be in business."

"I guess the person you want to serve first is the one who . . . who passed away, right?"

"Well, yes, the deceased and his or her survivors should be the first concern."

"But the deceased comes first, wouldn't you say?"

Mr. Lacey smiled and put a fatherly hand on his shoulder. "Are you interested in the business, Ozzy?"

"Well—"

"You know it when you have the call. Not many people do, but you know it when it happens." He started guiding Ozzy down the hallway.

"It *is* interesting, more than I thought—"

"Don't decide now. Just take your time, come back, and talk after things settle down."

Ozzy stopped and turned. "I'll definitely do that, Mr. Lacey, but what I want to talk about is Mom. About the way she wanted her funeral."

"You want to go over the arrangements?"

"I want to talk about Mom's arrangements." The words came gushing out of him. Slow down, he told himself. Grace under pressure. "Listen, Mr. Lacey, Mom really had her heart set on a cremation ceremony, not a burial. That was her real desire, and the whole thing's gotten out of hand with Sissy wanting her to be a Catholic, and Dad's so upset, he just—he's going along with it. But a burial wasn't what Mom wanted, you understand what I'm saying?"

"I think there's a little confusion, but that's natural at times like this."

"No, no, there's no confusion about what Mom wanted. Even Dad knows that."

"Why don't you sit down a minute—"

"No, it's not that."

"—I've got some Coke, 7-Up?"

Grace under pressure, grace under pressure. He let Mr. Lacey lead him to the couch, but he refused anything to drink. "It's like you said, Mr. Lacey, things have gotten confused, only not with me and Mom, but with Dad and Sissy. Now, I know you don't know that, but what I'm asking is, if there's a way to satisfy everybody with a funeral and still give Mom the ceremony she wanted, wouldn't you do it?"

"I'm not sure what you mean."

"Look, I know the funeral arrangements have gone too far to stop, I know that. But there is one way. If you could just deliver the, uh, the coffin, without Mom in it, then nobody would know, and it would work out fine. They could bury the coffin, and Mom could be cremated, and everybody would be happy."

Mr. Lacey stared at him like a sheep shot through the head. "Without the body?"

"Nobody would know, I swear. And I could pay you, too." He pulled out a roll of bills and thrust them forward. "See? A hundred and fifty dollars. Just for your trouble, not for anything else."

Mr. Lacey drew back from the money. "No, no . . ."

"Just for the actual cremation."

"I can't."

"If it's too much, I'll take some back."

Mr. Lacey shook his head. "Ozzy, you're upset . . ."

"No, I'm not. Look at my hand." He extended it. "It's steady as a rock. I'm totally calm, believe me. I just want to get Mom what she wanted."

Mr. Lacey stared at him a long moment and then sat down in the chair across from him. "All right, Ozzy. Explain it to me again."

For a moment he thought he'd done it. Mr. Lacey listened carefully and even asked a few questions. He believed him; Ozzy could see it in his face. When he was done, Mr. Lacey leaned back and smoothed his tie.

"Ozzy, I understand what you want to do, but I think you're going about it the wrong way. You've got to talk to your father—"

"I did, but he won't listen."

"He may be listening to his conscience, he may be."

"He's listening to Sissy, that's all."

"She's affected, too. All family members suffer from a loved one's passing, and their reactions sometime confuse us. Not everybody reacts the same way to grief, but, uh, they are the people you should deal with, because I can't help you. I can't—no, just listen a minute. I can't do what you ask, Ozzy. It's against the law, to begin with. I could lose my license and I could go to jail—"

But no one would know, Ozzy wanted say, but Mr. Lacey had his hand raised and his voice kept rumbling on, filling up every inch of the room.

"Secondly, it would be unethical to perpetrate a fraud like that. It would be a breach of faith in the trust invested in me by your father, and I'd be ashamed to even consider it—"

More than the words, Mr. Lacey's expression told him he had failed. Mr. Lacey cared, he could see that. But he cared about Dad and everybody, too.

"Finally, if I did what you ask, I couldn't live with myself, Ozzy. I hope you understand that."

Ozzy simply nodded. Of course he understood. He felt the same way about Mom's funeral. He remembered the way Mom looked in the dream, the way she smiled at him, letting him know he was special, letting him know she was counting on him. And he had failed her.

"I hope it works out," Mr. Lacey told him at the doorway.

So did Ozzy, but he didn't know how. He walked aimlessly downtown, feeling numb. He hadn't gotten much sleep the past two nights, and nothing felt right. Nothing felt like his life anymore. Even thinking about Dad and Lance and Sissy, it was like they were strangers. He hated the thought of seeing them again and wished he was some other person living some other life.

A Trailways bus sounded its horn as it turned into the station, momentarily blocking the sidewalk. Ozzy caught a glimpse of the sign above the windshield: New Orleans. His reflection in the silver panels jumped and danced as the bus passed in front of him. He thought about Mark Twain and Jack London and Ernest Hemingway. Walking slowly, as if in a trance, he entered the terminal and went to the ticket counter.

"How much is a ticket to New Orleans?"

The lady flipped open a book and ran her finger down the page.

"One-way or round-trip?"

Ozzy felt his stomach tingle. "One-way."

"Eighty-nine ninety-five, including tax."

"And that's the bus out there?"

"That's the one."

He stepped outside and looked around. The buildings downtown looked cleaner and brighter than they ever had before and the mountains were closer and the air was crackling. People were getting on the bus with paper cups of coffee and sandwiches wrapped in cellophane and their voices were loud and vibrating. The whole world was loud and vibrating, and he felt as if he were standing on the high dive leaning forward, forward, forward . . .

He went inside and bought a ticket to New Orleans.

Chapter 9

THE MOUNTAINS LASTED A LONG TIME, rising and falling behind them. It was really the bus that was going up and down, moving over the elongated rolling plains that spread toward Kansas like dying waves. When the bus went downhill, the mountains seemed to sink into the ground, leaving the horizon flat. But as they climbed to the crest of another ridge, the peaks would rise, sharp and white, as if cut into the sky with a knife. Ozzy marveled that the mountains could last so long. Two or three times he was convinced they had disappeared for good, but then the bus would mount a higher hill and there they were, as if unwilling to let him go. Finally there were no more high ridges, and Ozzy was on his own.

He turned and settled back into his seat. The bus was only half full, so there was no one in the seat beside him. It was just as well. He was exhausted and his mind was blank and he didn't want to talk to anybody. He just wanted to sit there and stare out the window at the brown earth and patchy snow and the red and blue interstate highway signs that told him he was on his way somewhere. The big seat was comfortable, and there was heat coming from a narrow grille at the floor. He took off his shoes and socks, damp from the snow, and shoved them close to the grille. The heat made him drowsy. He took off Gary's jacket, bunched it into a pillow, and rested his head on it. He knew he should think about what he was doing, make some plans or something, but he was too tired. He brought his feet up and let the motion of the bus rock him to sleep.

He dreamed about Mom and birthdays and going to zoos and playing Monopoly and licking the spoon and listening to bedtime stories and a thousand other things, all mixed up except the last one, the dream about the Mars bars. It was when he was a kid and they were living at Clark Air Force Base in the Philippines. He was with Mom, shopping at the PX. He showed her a candy bar, but she wouldn't buy it for him, so when he found himself alone, he stuck it in his pocket. Later, when they went through the checkout counter, the clerk spotted the Mars bar and said to Mom, "I think you forgot something."

Mom didn't get mad or anything. She bought two boxes of Mars bars and took them home. Then she sat him down on the couch and said, "Do you feel wonderful, Ozzy?"

"What do you mean?"

"Do you feel wonderful?"

"No," he said slowly, trying to figure out the right answer.

"Maybe a candy bar will help." She opened the box of Mars bars.

"That's okay."

"No, go ahead. Let's see how good it makes you feel."

Ozzy ate the Mars bar while Mom watched. When he was finished, she said, "How's that?"

"Fine."

"Do you feel wonderful now?"

"I guess."

"Eat another one."

"Mom . . ."

"Let's see. Maybe two will make you feel twice as good."

Ozzy ate lots of Mars bars before he got sick. Afterward Mom said, "There aren't enough candy bars in the world to make you feel wonderful, Ozzy. You can't buy enough or steal enough. And without feeling wonderful, what's the point of it all?"

The bus jolted to a stop and he woke.

"This is Salina, folks," the driver yelled. "We'll be here about forty-five minutes for those of you who want to eat."

Ozzy struggled into a sitting position and was surprised to see it was already dusk. A thin ribbon of pink ran along the horizon, topped by a deep blue sky that darkened to black in the east. His neck was stiff, and there was perspiration on his cheek from the slick material of the ski parka. He couldn't believe he'd slept nearly eight hours.

Ozzy got out and went with the other passengers to the Sunflower Café. His shoes were were warm and stiff from lying next to the heating vent, and Gary's ski parka was all wrinkled, but nobody paid any attention. The café was pretty crowded because, in addition to his bus, there was another bus going to Chicago. He found a spot at the counter between a family with three kids and a thin, sandy-haired man chewing a toothpick. Ozzy ordered a dinner special because it looked like the best deal. He was going to have to watch his money until he got to Paris. That was his plan. Paris. Like Thomas Wolfe said, "You can't go home again." And he couldn't. Not after what he had said, not after what he had done.

Sitting in the Sunflower Café, Ozzy felt the weight of destiny settle over his shoulders. As a future famous writer he was no longer able to live in a small town like Capitol. There wasn't enough intellectual stimulation or people who shared the same artistic vision. Paris was the place to go, and he had a plan for how to get there. When they reached New Orleans, he'd go to the wharf district and ship out on the first freighter going to Europe. He would take a job as a cabin boy or a dishwasher, anything. He didn't care if they strapped him to the bow to look for icebergs, just as long as he got to Paris. He'd save some money so that he could rent a garret and buy a used typewriter, and then he'd write the book—the book that would make Mom famous and Sissy and Dad despicable. A hundred years from now, when everybody was dead, people would remember Mom the way he did, not the way Sissy and Dad did. Ozzy smiled grimly. Finally he had some power. All he had to do was get to Paris.

He paid the bill and left a quarter tip, which made

him feel guilty because it wasn't even ten percent, but he figured the waitress was making more money than he was. He went to a drugstore and bought a thirty-nine-cent spiral notepad. The front part would be his literary journal, and the back would be his expense record. He opened the front cover and wrote, "Salina—flat as Dad's jokes." Then he flipped it over and inside the back cover, wrote, "Ticket = $89.95; Dinner + tax + tip = 4.65; this notebook = 39¢."

Back at the bus he found half a dozen people lined up to get aboard and a young woman going down the line, talking to each person. He noticed her right away because she was wearing a short white fur coat over blue jeans and she was pretty. She had brown hair and excited green eyes and hands that flipped through the air like mittens pinned to a kid's coat. They were sexy hands, model's hands. He watched the way she used them as she moved down the line.

" 'Scuse me, are y'all going to New Orleans?" It was some kind of Southern accent that made her seem even more exotic.

"Sorry, honey," a fat lady carrying a wicker basket told her. "I get off at Oak City."

Ozzy couldn't figure it out. She didn't look like a bus passenger, all dressed up in a white fur coat, but she did have a bunch of clothes stuffed into a red fishnet bag she had on her shoulder. She came up to an older couple in front of him.

" 'Scuse me, folks, y'all be going to New Orleans?"

The man had a thin face with heavy lines across the forehead. He frowned slightly and said, "That's right."

She leaned forward, her eyes intent, her hands pulling the air between them close. "Then you can do me a big favor. I need a loan of twenty dollars to get me a ticket to New Orleans, where I'll pay you back as soon as we get there, and in the meantime, you can keep this here double-diamond ring as collateral."

Up close, Ozzy could see she wasn't much older than he was. He decided she wasn't so much pretty as cute. She had a heart-shaped face with high cheekbones, a short, perky nose, and thin, no-nonsense lips that were softened by a rounded chin. Her hair was more red than he thought, a dark copper brown with sweeping waves.

The bus driver came out of the terminal and headed toward them. When she saw him, the girl started talking even faster. "My momma lives in New Orleans and she'll be there to pay you back, I swear—"

The driver waved his hand as he approached. "Go on, now. What'd we tell you about bothering the passengers?"

"I got a right to talk to these people."

"Not on the premises. We told you once—" He took her arm, but she pulled away, her eyes flashing.

"Don't you touch my brand-new coat."

"Then move along now, before that dispatcher calls the police."

"Are *you* going to loan me the twenty dollars?"

"Lady—" The driver looked past her to the terminal where the agent was watching just inside the door. The driver waved to him, motioning him to come out, but when the girl saw what was happening, she moved away.

"All right, all right, I'm going."

She disappeared around the rear of the bus, and people started getting back aboard. Ozzy smiled to himself. This was the real world, all right. Weird people, crazy situations, unpredictability lurking around every corner. He almost wished he'd left home years ago.

"Psssst."

It sounded like air escaping from a tire, but it was the girl, motioning to him from behind the bus. Ozzy glanced around. The driver was busy helping an old lady put tags on her luggage.

"Psssst!" The girl motioned to him like an angry traffic cop. He left the crowd and went over. As soon as he got close, she said in a low, intense voice, "Are *you* goin' to New Orleans?"

Ozzy nodded, and she grabbed his arm and pulled him behind the bus. "I'm sorry, but I've got to get out of town and I need twenty dollars to get me a ticket home. Now, I've got collateral for a loan." She thrust out her hand to display a wedding ring with two small diamonds. "This here's a genuine eighteen-carat double-diamond ring, which you can hold on to until we get to New Orleans. That way you got a guarantee you'll get your money back, now how does that sound?"

Ozzy didn't know what to say. The way she was whispering and looking around, it was like a big adventure. Like being in a James Bond movie, only he wasn't sure what part he was supposed to play.

"Come on, come on." She glanced around nervously. "Before this thing leaves."

"I don't have much money—" Ozzy began.

"Damn." She stamped her foot. "Ain't there one solitary person in this world going to loan me twenty dollars? Now, look." She pulled him to the edge of the bus and pointed at a passenger. "You see that woman there? You go find out if she's going to New Orleans. Find somebody who's going to New Orleans and send them over here. You can at least do that, can't you?"

Ozzy was intrigued. There was a way she had of talking that pulled the whole world in and made everything terrible and important. "Why do you need to get to New Orleans?"

"Never you mind. Just get that kindly-looking woman to come over so's I can talk to her."

"I've got twenty dollars," he said. The words just popped out, because he'd already made up his mind not to give her any money. It was exciting and all that, but he didn't trust her for one minute. Not a girl who wore a fur coat in a bus station. And now he'd gone and offered her the money. She grabbed his hand and gave it a quick squeeze.

"You're an angel. I swear, my momma's going to be right there at the bus station to pay you back. Now, you keep this double-diamond ring so everything's on the up-and-up."

Ozzy found himself handing over the twenty dollars. The girl kept talking, and he wondered if she was on drugs or something, she had so much energy. "That man at the counter's like to drop over dead when he sees me come back with the money."

He stood outside the terminal and watched through the window as she went to the ticket booth. He had this vision of her walking right past the counter and out the side door into the street. That was probably how she made her money, buying rings by the dozen at Sears or someplace and selling them in bus stations to dumb people who believed her. He looked at the ring she pressed into his hand, but it was too dark to tell much about it. He moved into the light, held up the ring, and turned it slowly. The facets caught the light and sent it dancing. He'd never compared diamonds to glass, but these looked real.

The announcement came over the PA system: "Last call for Trailways Express Coach Service to Wichita, Oklahoma City, Dallas–Fort Worth, Houston, Baton Rouge, and New Orleans. Last boarding call."

Ozzy looked up, and the girl was gone. The counter was empty. He felt the bottom drop out of his stomach. Less than twenty-four hours on his own, and already he'd been taken. He was a fool, an idiot, a jerk-off. He was too stupid ever to be a famous writer. Then he saw her, stepping aboard the bus. The driver saw him and called out, "You on this bus, son?"

"Yes, sir." He hurried over.

"Best get aboard," the driver said as he mounted the steps. Ozzy felt a tingle of excitement. She was on the bus after all, his mystery woman. Now they would sit together and talk and he'd find out why she was going to New Orleans and why she didn't have any money and why she was wearing a fur coat in a bus station. On *Miami Vice* and *L.A. Law* it was always the prostitutes who wore fur coats at night. Maybe she was one of the them, only not the scuzzy kind they had in Denver, but a high-class lady whose family fortune had been dissipated by an unscrupulous uncle and the only way they could keep the family art treasures was if she sold her body to corporate executives. That's why she was leaving Salina. She was going to New Orleans, where nobody would know her and the executives had more money. This was right at the start of her legendary career, so she didn't have VD and herpes and AIDS and all the rotten things people ran into in sex-education films. She was still fresh and virginal, like an unplucked rose. And Ozzy had just done her the biggest favor of her life . . .

She was getting settled near the back of the bus opposite the driver's side. The fishnet bag was on the seat beside her, and she was taking off her coat. When she saw Ozzy, she gave him a quick smile.

"I sure thank you for helping me out."

"No problem," Ozzy said smoothly. He motioned the seat with the bag on it. "You mind if I . . . ?"

She paused, glanced around, and saw that there were other double seats vacant.

"To tell you the truth, I'm bone-tired and I'm fixing to lay myself out here and get some sleep. But there's plenty of seats right behind here, so . . ." She gave a little shrug, then shoved the bag up against the window and used it as a pillow. She tucked her feet up on the second seat and spread the coat over her like a blanket.

The bus gave a jolt and began to back up. Ozzy took a seat directly behind the girl, where he could see the streetlights glisten off her hair as they drove through town. That was all he could see—just this clump of brown hair that glowed copper every time a streetlight hit it. He wondered if she was really tired or did she think he was some kind of dork and didn't want to sit next to him?

Ozzy rested his head against the window and

thought about how weird it was going to be not going to school tomorrow. That was the only bad thing—he wouldn't get his diploma. It seemed a shame, after spending his entire life in school, to stop short just five months away. It was a good thing he wanted to do famous writing, since not that many careers let you get away without a high school diploma. He remembered reading in *Famous Authorship* how Jack London walked out of class when his English teacher tried to tell him how to write. Really a stupid teacher, trying to tell Jack London how to write.

Thinking about school made him remember Lisa and their miserable date. It seemed like a million years ago that he was rubbing her jelly-roll stomach and watching Anouk Aimee's lips pout at him from the screen. Maybe he would meet Anouk Aimee's daughter in Paris. At least he wouldn't have to face Lisa again, that was one good thing.

Ozzy was still awake when the bus reached Wichita, a little after midnight. Wichita was bigger than he thought, and a lot of people got on, including some man in a plaid suit and tan overcoat. He had gray hair and the face of an actor in an old folks' home. He stood for a moment, looked the bus over, then went right up to where the girl was sleeping and tapped her on the leg.

"Excuse me, Little Miss, can I sit down?"

Ozzy couldn't believe it. She was obviously asleep, but this guy didn't care at all. He just came right up and started banging on her foot.

"If you don't mind, I'm sleeping."

He was happy to hear her voice; it was familiar. But the guy didn't pay any attention. "I'm sorry, but I've got to sit somewhere, and that somewhere looks good right here." He slid her feet to one side and sat down in one fluid motion. It took the girl by surprise. She sat up and said angrily, "Would you mind? This is my seat."

"There's two seats here, Little Miss. One for you and one for me."

"Well, just you go sit somewhere else."

"Now, don't be like that. I can be a very entertaining gentleman if you give me half a chance."

"I'm giving you three seconds to get up from there and go find somewhere else to sit."

"I've got to sit beside somebody, and I always make it the prettiest little girl I can find."

Ozzy nearly barfed. Did this guy really think anybody would fall for that "pretty little girl" stuff? It was so hokey, he couldn't believe it. Of course, it was good material. He might want to write about a real jerk someday. He reached for his notepad as the girl stood up.

"You can sit over . . ." She looked around, but the man was right—there were no more double seats vacant. She saw Ozzy looking at her, and suddenly her expression changed. "No, don't," she said quickly. "It's okay, Raymond. I'll sit with you. No, don't get up."

Ozzy looked behind him, but there was nobody he could see. Meanwhile the girl turned back to her seat, picked up her bag, and was trying to move past the guy. "Excuse me."

"Where're you going?"

Instead of answering, she looked over his head, at Ozzy. Her eyes grew wide with fear. "No, no! Don't hit him. He won't make trouble. Just stay there, Raymond.

Stay there." She turned to the man in the seat. "Oh Christ, hurry up, let me by."

Ozzy could see the back of the man's head rise as he squeezed back to let her past. She moved quickly into the seat beside Ozzy, still talking. "Sorry, honey, he didn't mean no harm. Let me just sit here with you so's *Daddy* don't get worried. You know what a temper he's got, and since he's still *asleep* in the *front of the bus,* I'd hate to wake him up. You relax here, now, or you'll end up like Daddy, spending all your time in the penitentiary just 'cause you got mad at somebody. I baked me enough biscuits to last a lifetime and I ain't going to start again with you if you break somebody's head open on a bus." She leaned over close to Ozzy and whispered, "Sorry. I would've told the bus driver, but I already had a run-in with him."

"It's okay," he whispered back. But he kept his eyes on the back of the seat, expecting at any moment to see the guy turn around with a pair of brass knuckles on his fist. But nothing happened. Not even the top of the man's head was visible anymore.

The girl put her seat into the reclined position, tucked her legs up under her, and fitted the coat over her shoulders from the front. She caught his eye, indicated the back of the seat, then made a face and stuck out her tongue. Ozzy grinned. She leaned over and whispered, "My name's Maysie Perlmutter."

She turned her ear to him, and Ozzy caught a whiff of something that wasn't perfume, but more like a faint shampoo smell. "Ozzy Mills," he whispered.

"Thanks a second time."

She settled into the seat, drew her coat tight, and

closed her eyes. Ozzy watched as her head began to nod. Every once in a while she'd jerk her head back up, and then it would begin slipping forward again. Finally she shifted around so that her head was wedged against Ozzy's seat back and closed her eyes. Ozzy couldn't believe she was falling asleep right there beside him. It was such a vulnerable thing to do, falling asleep beside a total stranger. He'd never been this close to a sleeping girl before. He leaned forward so that he could watch it happen.

The first thing he noticed was that Maysie wasn't as cute asleep as she was awake. It wasn't because her face was blue from the lights down near the floor, it was something else. Everything was still cute individually, but it didn't go together anymore. It was like her mouth was from one cute girl's face and her nose from another and her chin from another cute girl, but none of it was from the same girl. There was something missing. Then he realized—it was her eyes. Those intense green eyes were like an energy force that molded everything together into one complete face, and when she was asleep, it was like a switch had been turned off. He wondered if it worked that way with everybody. When he shut his eyes, did his face become more like pieces of jigsaw than a whole face? He leaned back and tried it. He shut his eyes and tried to imagine what his face looked like. He thought about each part—his nose, his eyes, his ears, his mouth—all hanging out there separately. He had this image of a cartoon show where some dopey character swallows an exploding cigar and when it goes off, all the parts of his face go flying off in all directions.

Ozzy didn't like the feeling he got when he thought about his face in pieces, so he went back to thinking about it as a whole. Besides, the only way he could tell what he actually looked like asleep would be to put a camera over his bed with a timer on it. He opened his eyes and looked at Maysie again and was surprised to see she was sleeping with her mouth open. He didn't know girls did that. He thought they had a biological protection against doing crude things like burping out loud and sleeping with their mouths open. Maysie even had a damp spot of saliva on the shoulder of her blouse. He got out his literary notebook and angled it toward the light.

"Girl sleeps with mouth open," he wrote carefully. He heard a faint sound next to him. "Girl snores!" The whole thing was a revelation, but what surprised him most was that he wasn't grossed out by it. Usually he couldn't stand crude things like guys in PE spitting on the track when they ran laps or girls who clipped their fingernails in the cafeteria. Those kinds of things usually drove him up the wall, but with Maysie, they actually had a kind of a charm. He hoped it was because she looked so sweet and vulnerable and not due to any crudity perversion that was sneaking up on him.

He leaned back, put his head against the window, and looked up at the night sky. The stars rotated slowly, first one way, then back the other, as the bus wound its way toward Oklahoma. A girl was asleep beside him and the night was magic. It felt good to be alive.

Chapter 10

MAYSIE was putting on makeup when he woke up. She held a compact in front of her face and stared into a tiny mirror as she brushed mascara on her eyelashes. Ozzy watched without moving. She used short, quick little strokes with a blink between each one. Her concentration was so total, she didn't notice him watching, and Ozzy felt like he was invisible. He remembered the game he and King Shipley used to play. King Shipley was his childhood friend who moved to Charlottesville when his dad got a job at the University of Virginia. The game they played was more of a question than a game:

"Would you rather be able to fly or to be invisible?"

"To be able to fly," King would say.

"To be invisible," Ozzy would say. Then they'd argue about which would be best. Ozzy still thought about it sometimes, but the answer was different depending on his mood. If it was some kind of special day —like in the middle of winter, when the warm chinook winds came and melted the ice and made the air feel like silk, or in the summer, when the sky was so blue and the clouds were so white that it was like living in a Van Gogh painting—when it was a day like that that made him feel glorious, he wished he could fly. But as he got older, more and more he could see the advantages of being invisible, especially when it came to watching girls get dressed in their bedrooms. That's how he felt leaning up against the window of the bus with his eyes half open—like he was watching Maysie in her bedroom.

It wasn't until she tucked the mascara brush into its tube and went to put it away that she noticed he was awake.

"Good morning, sleepyhead."

"Hi." Ozzy sat up.

"You was sleeping so sound, I thought sure you'd miss out on Dallas."

"Are we in Texas?"

"Deep in the heart of." She pointed out the window. The land was flat and dry and brown, but in the distance, tall buildings rose dark against the sky. Off to the right, a shallow river valley paralleled the road, first angling close and then swinging away to make room for half-finished housing developments. The only trees were scrub oak and mesquite and skeleton-looking things that grew along the river valley. Texas wasn't exactly a Garden of Eden.

As Maysie took out her eyeliner, she noticed Ozzy put his finger on the window. "It's real, all right," she said.

"I was just testing to see how cold it was. There's no snow or anything."

She raised the pencil to her eyelid. "Ain't no snow, but it's still cold. Cold in the winter and hot in the summer, that's Dallas for you."

"Are you from Dallas?"

"No, thank you, but I spent three months in Greenville, so I know it well enough."

Ozzy didn't know where Greenville was, but that was the way with Southern people. If they knew where a place was, they figured everybody else did, too. He looked around the bus. It was still about three-quarters full. Across the aisle from Maysie a bald man was reading a book, and in front of him, someone's feet were sticking out in the aisle. Ozzy wondered who was in front of them, if it was the same jerk as last night. He craned up but couldn't see anything. He turned to Maysie and said in a low voice, "Is he still . . . ?"

"No." She shook her head. "That old jaygool got off back at Oklahoma City."

He stared at her. "That what?"

"That old boy that tried to pick me up last night? Isn't that who you're talking about?"

"Yeah."

"He got off at Oak City." She snapped the compact shut and stuffed it into a leather purse. She was wearing a green blouse that brought out the color of her eyes, and now that she was awake and moving around, her whole face looked cute again. But he was still thinking about what she called the guy last night. A "jaygool," was it? It was like going to a foreign country, talking to Maysie.

She put her hands behind her neck, lifted her hair, and began twisting back and forth.

"I got a crick in my neck," she explained. Her elbows were high in the air, and Ozzy couldn't help noticing the way her breasts showed through, the nipples bunched up like marbles against the fabric.

"So how come you're going to New Orleans?" he asked, partly to find out and partly so he'd have a reason to keep watching her nipples.

"Me and my husband had a fight, so I took off. I'm gonna stay with my momma until I get me a cheap lawyer who can sue that animal up one side and down the other." She dropped her hands to her lap and turned to Ozzy. "How about you?"

"Uh, I took off, too. I'm going to Paris."

Maysie frowned. "Paris, Texas?"

"No. Paris, France."

"French Paris? That's where you're going, French Paris?"

"As soon as I get a job on a ship or something. That's why I'm going to New Orleans, to get a job to get to Paris." Ozzy didn't want to stare, but there was something about her face, the attention she paid to everything he said, that made it hard to look away.

"You got family in French Paris, is that it?"

"No."

"You going to school over there?"

"No, I dropped out of school yesterday. I'm going to Paris to be a writer. A famous author, you know—like Hemingway and Faulkner and Fitzgerald. They all went to Paris to learn how to write."

"I thought them old boys wrote in English."

"Oh, they did. It's not that they wrote in French, it's just that Paris is a very nurturing environment for—" The slow smile creeping across her face stopped him. "What?"

"Y'all don't have to tell me why you're going to New Orleans. Just say, 'Mind your own business, Maysie,' and I'll shut up." She was still grinning, and Ozzy realized she thought he was making everything up.

"No, that's why. That's really the reason I'm going."

"All right, all right." She waved the air as if clearing it of smoke. "Let me just ask you one thing, then. How come, if you're going to French Paris, which happens to be the fashion capital of the world, you're dressed up like you're going to a funeral?"

Ozzy was stunned. How did she know? And then he realized she was talking about his black shirt and pants—his writer's outfit—not Mom. He told her about the writer's persona and how you had to think and act and dress like a famous writer if you wanted to be one. "It's like this form of literary self-realization that these two guys, Hogarth and Ratliff, came up with. And the earlier you begin, the bigger your fame potential, so that's why I do it. That's why I wear black."

"But that's not all writers, is it? They don't all wear one color or dress like they're Lash La Rue or somebody."

"Not many of them do it. Just Tom Wolfe and a couple of others. It's a new technique, really." Ozzy was pleased. Maysie didn't make fun of it like Dad or get bored with it like Gary or try to talk him out of it or anything. She seemed very interested.

"But Rosemary Rogers, she don't wear the same color dress day in and day out?"

"Who?"

"Rosemary Rogers. You don't know who she is?"

"No."

Maysie looked disappointed. "She writes all them Windswept romances you see in the Safeway store. You must have seen them. You can't hardly buy a can of tomato soup without seeing some new book she wrote."

Ozzy smiled at her lack of sophistication. He felt like a Gothic duke talking to a quilt-skirted peasant girl. "Books like that aren't real literature."

"Why not?"

"Well, because they don't deal with big themes. They're emotional-type books."

Maysie's eyes widened in surprise. "What do you mean they don't deal with big themes? They're all about life and death and sickness and health and whether people are going to mess around or stay pure. Where's anything more important than that?"

"It's not just life and death, it's like . . ." He hesitated. Maysie's steadfast gaze was disconcerting. "Like philosophical implications. Symbols of man's condition. You know. Things like mountain climbing and deep-sea fishing and bullfighting."

"Bullfighting! What kind of theme is that except Mexican?"

"I mean Spanish bullfighting. Where people get gored and it's very serious and symbolic."

She tossed her head. "Now, that's the dumbest thing I ever heard. Who gives a woollybugger what happens to some old bull or anybody stupid enough to wave flags at him?"

"All right, then, war. War is a big theme. War and peace, that's what makes books into real literature."

She looked at him a long moment and then said, "What about *Alice in Wonderland*?"

"Well, sure," Ozzy fumbled. "There are exceptions, sure . . ."

"All right, you think up what they are while I go brush my teeth." She dug down in her purse and pulled out a pink toothbrush with a gold-speckled handle and toilet paper wrapped around its bristles. "Y'all watch my stuff, okay?"

As she moved into the aisle, he got a side view of her lower body. Maysie had a nice rear end and a flat stomach, the exact opposite of Lisa's. She had the kind of stomach that made his hand tingle when he thought of touching it. The bald man across the aisle thought so, too. He put down his book and let his eyes roam around on Maysie's jeans as she moved away. Then he caught Ozzy's eye and gave a little wink before going back to his book. It surprised Ozzy and made him feel annoyed and pleased at the same time. On the one hand, he was annoyed that this bald guy would scope her out in such an obvious way, like he was checking out a new car or something. On the other hand, the guy realized Ozzy was doing the same thing, and the wink made him feel like he was part of some secret organization or hidden brotherhood. After all, Maysie wasn't *his* wife or anything. She was some other guy's wife, a guy she was going to divorce up one side and down the other. He wondered what her husband had done to make her run off. Maybe he was an alcoholic slob or perverted wife swapper or he ignored her and watched football games day and night. That kind of stuff drove women crazy. One thing Ozzy knew, he was going to have some great material by the time he reached Paris. He pulled out his notepad and started a new heading: "Low-Class Phrases." Underneath, he wrote, "Jaygool—what does it mean?" and then, "Woollybugger—is this a cuss word?" He tried to think if there was anything else Maysie had said that was exotic and low-class and Southern.

"Hey, Dad, look." A crewcut boy two seats away stood up and pointed. "There's a car on fire."

Ozzy pressed his head against the window. Up ahead, a column of dark, black smoke drifted lazily over the highway. The bus slowed down, and he saw a yellow van on the opposite side of the freeway. The van was stopped on the side of the road with its hood up, dark, angry smoke pouring from the engine compartment. Maysie came back and leaned across him to peer out the window.

"What is it?"

"There's a car on fire."

"Jesus, look at that thing." She pressed closer, and Ozzy felt her breast against his arm. He froze. He didn't see the van anymore. All his senses were concentrated on that one spot on his arm. Maysie was too excited to notice.

"What are they doing? They're going to get blowed up."

Ozzy forced himself to concentrate. There were three people running around the van, trying to put the fire out. They were young, two guys and a girl, and the way they tried to put out the fire was by scooping up handfuls of dirt and throwing it on the engine.

"Did you see it, Dad?" the kid in front kept yelling. "Did you see it?"

Maysie sat down. "That thing is going to blow sky-high, and those poor people are going to get killed."

She looked so worried, as if her baby were lying on the railroad tracks or something, that Ozzy would have said anything to make her happy. He shook his head. "It looked like a new van, and they have fire-protection cutoff switches on them. Like in your house, where you have smoke detectors."

"We live in a trailer. We don't have no smoke detectors."

"You live in a trailer?"

"A house trailer. We got us a ten-wide ABC, but it don't have no smoke detectors. Supposed to be, but we never got around to it yet." She glanced out the window as a police car with its lights flashing passed going the other way. "There they go. Good." She settled back into her seat.

"My granddad lived in a house trailer," Ozzy said.

"He did? Was he a tower man?"

"A what?"

"Did he work water towers?

"No, he worked in the post office."

"Good for him. I wouldn't wish water tower work on a dog. Never in one place long enough to know which way's up and which way's down."

"Is that what your dad did? Built water towers?"

She gave her head a brisk shake. "No, Daddy did

everything, none of it very long or very good. Brandt's the one. He's my husband and he's a pusher on the water towers. That's what the argument was all about. I told him before we was married, I wouldn't bring up no family moving around from one town to the other, never knowing anybody long enough to say hello before it was time to say good-bye. That's the way I was brought up, hopping from one Gulf town to the other, Pensacola to Port Arthur, and I wouldn't put my own kids through that kind of niggerliving for all the money in Fort Knox. That's what I told Brandt the very first time we met, I said—" She noticed Ozzy's expression and stopped. "What?"

He leaned forward and said in a low voice, "There's some of them in the bus."

"Who? Who're you talking about?"

"Some black people."

"I know there's black people on the bus. So what?"

He looked around, wishing she would keep her voice down. "You used the *N* word."

"The what? Ozzy, what're you talking about?"

He leaned over and whispered carefully, "You called them niggers."

Thinking she understood, he gave her a "see what I mean?" look. But she looked at him and said, "I didn't call anybody a nigger."

She said it in a low voice, but the word echoed in his ears like it had been announced over the loudspeaker.

"Shhh. Shhhh." He waved her silent.

"What is the matter with you?" she demanded. "You think I'm crazy? I don't call people words like that."

He leaned forward again. "You said 'niggerliving,' remember?"

"So what? That ain't calling people niggers."

"Shhh. Shhhh."

"Ozzy, don't do me like this—"

"It's not a nice word," he insisted. "It's an insult word. People throw rocks and burn cities when they hear that word."

"Now you're being silly."

"No, really—"

"Listen, now." She leaned forward, her eyes dark and serious. "I never did finish my high school diploma, and I don't aim to be no writer, but I'm not trash. I'm not ignorant. And I'm not out to make other people into ignorant trash by the calling of names. I don't call black people niggers and I don't call Mexicans spics and I don't call Jews Jews, so you can just stop your lecture right here and now." She nodded out the window. "That there's the Reunion Tower, in case you're interested."

He looked out the window. They were already in Dallas, leaving the freeway and heading downtown. The Reunion Tower stuck up above the other building like a giant golf ball on a three-legged tee. It was impressive and all that, but Ozzy was still thinking about Maysie and what she'd said. From the way she clamped her mouth shut when she ended the conversation, he knew her mind was made up. As long as she didn't actually *call* somebody a nigger, she didn't see anything wrong with it. It was too bad, really. Here she was, this cute girl, especially when she was awake, with a dynamite body and a fun-type personality, but she had a limited education and didn't understand artistic concepts and thought she could fling around insult words as long as she didn't actually use them on people.

His attention was caught by what looked like a monster white concrete block. As they got closer, he saw it was actually two concrete walls set off the ground on short, square legs.

"That's the Kennedy Memorial," Maysie said. "On account of Dallas is where he was killed. And down there," she pointed, "is the building where old Lee Harvey Oswald hid out and waited for him."

Ozzy craned to see as the bus turned the corner and the memorial slipped from sight. So that was it, he thought, the place where President Kennedy died. Thinking about it reminded him of Mom's death, and he felt a quick burst of sadness. It was weird how not thinking about her made things seem normal, but as soon as he stopped to focus on what had happened, this sick feeling would come over him.

Ozzy wondered what was happening at home. By now they would have talked to Gary and maybe even Old Man Lacey. He hoped Old Man Lacey hadn't told them about the bribe. But he probably did. Undertakers were like teachers and probably told parents anything they wanted to know. And then there was the police. They would be in on it by now. He had this image of them circulating his picture, talking to gas station attendants and pawnshop owners.

"Have you ever seen this boy before?"

"I don't know. Is that Ozzy Mills?"

"We ask the questions, sir, you just give us the answers. Have you seen him or not?"

"No, I swear I haven't."

"All right, but don't leave town until we find him."

Yes, Ozzy thought, they would be looking for him now, all right. Remembering the devastated look on Dad's face, he felt a stab of remorse. It wasn't that he wanted to cause any more pain, but what else could he do? Nobody listened to him. Nobody would let him do the last thing he could for Mom, which was respect her wishes about the funeral. If only he could turn back the clock. If only—

"Dallas, folks," the driver announced. "We'll have an hour before we leave. One hour."

It was ten o'clock, and Ozzy hadn't had breakfast. He was hungry but wasn't sure he wanted to eat breakfast with a prejudiced girl, even if she was cute. He decided to wait until Maysie got off the bus and then find a place where he could eat alone. But he changed his mind as soon as she stood up and flashed her Freeway jeans in his face. Freeway was the label above the right pocket, and the design showed a road with yellow lines disappearing in the distance. A Calvin Klein label would have been too fancy, and Levi's would have been too plain, but something about Freeway was just right. He stood up and said, "You want to eat breakfast?"

"I'm not hungry," she said easily. "But I'll get me a cup of coffee."

"Great," he said. He grabbed Gary's coat and followed her down the aisle, keeping an eye on the Freeway label all the way.

Chapter 11

THE TERMINAL was one big, polished room with a white floor and shiny red plastic chairs chained back-to-back in rows down the center. Everywhere you looked were posters of Trailways buses zooming across America with the slogan "Go Big Red." He turned to Maysie.

"I'll bet somebody got a hundred thousand dollars for thinking that up."

"Thinking what up?"

"That slogan, 'Go Big Red.' Some writer thought that up. Some ad writer who lives in New York and gets paid a ton of money to think up things like 'Go Big Red.' "

Maysie turned to stare at the sign. "Them three little old words? *Go* and *big* and *red*? Somebody got a hundred thousand dollars for them?"

"Maybe not that much, but ten or twenty thousand, anyway. They get paid a lot of money, ad writers."

Maysie was wearing her white fur coat, and Ozzy felt a kind of pride that he was standing beside her where a lot of people could see them together. They probably thought he was making it with her. They thought he knew what she looked like naked. He imagined them imagining him, hot and virile on top of Maysie's glistening body, both of them twisting away on top of tangled sheets . . .

Maysie let out a low whistle. She was still staring at the poster. "Ten thousand dollars for three puny words. I don't believe it."

"It's not just the words, it's how you say them. 'Big Red Go' wouldn't be the same as 'Go Big Red.' "

"Then how much would 'Big Red Go' be worth?"

"It's not worth anything. That's the challenge with being an author. You've got to come up with the right words in the right order or it's nothing."

She looked at him with a mixture of suspicion and admiration. "Then you got your work cut out for you, huh?"

They went to a restaurant next to the terminal called Jimbo's. It was fixed up in a fake Western style, with the lights hung from wagon wheels and varnished wooden tables and chairs with brands on them. They sat in a booth next to a window. The smell of bacon and fresh coffee mingled with cigarette smoke was real, even if the mounted bull horns above each booth were plastic.

The waitress was a chunky lady with a beehive hairdo and smudged lipstick. She wore a brown and white uniform with a pencil-thin tie that made her look like a grandma riverboat gambler.

"What can I get you folks?"

Maysie motioned for him to go ahead, so Ozzy ordered a Western omelet. The waitress made two marks on her pad.

"Toast or biscuits?"

"Uh, biscuits."

"Coffee to start?"

"Sure."

Normally he didn't drink coffee, but now that he was on his own and sitting across from Maysie, it made him feel more like an adult. Besides, if he was going to be a famous writer, he had to be a coffee addict. All the great writers were coffee addicts as well as alcoholics.

The waitress made another mark and turned to Maysie. "What about you, miss?"

"Just coffee, with plenty of cream and sugar."

"Nothing to eat?"

"Nope." The waitress left, and Maysie grinned. "She thinks you're my fancy man."

"What?"

"That there waitress. She thinks you're my fancy man. You know—my stud."

"She does?"

Ozzy looked after the waitress, but there was nothing in her square back or brisk walk that said what she thought. All the sexy thoughts he'd been having about Maysie came crowding back into his brain, and he kept his eyes on the sugar bowl. Maysie laughed, quick and sharp like a spoon tapping a wineglass.

"Why, Ozzy, you're blushing."

"No, I'm not."

"Sure you are. You got a red line creeping up your face like a July thermometer."

"It's not me," he protested. "It's probably you wearing a fur coat in the middle of a bus terminal, that's what gave her ideas."

She looked down. "What's the matter with my coat? It's the best thing I own."

"What it looks like, you know. Wearing it during the day in this kind of place."

She leaned forward, tilted her head to one side, and whispered, "You think I look like a lady of easy virtue?"

"Not me, but maybe these other people . . ." He let the thought hang. He didn't want to insult Maysie or anything. But she leaned back and grinned at the thought.

"I'll tell you, when I was a little girl, I used to think that was the way to go. I seen these women on the street corner wearing all kinds of fancy clothes, high heels, spangled skirts, low-cut silk blouses, and fur coats up to their ears. I had me all kinds of visions of lying around on satin sheets waiting for some rich man to discover me, a pearl among the swine, and pluck me out and carry me off to some mansion in the sky."

Ozzy couldn't help smiling. It wasn't just the way her eyes glazed over or her hands painted pictures in the air as she described all this stuff, it was that Maysie's girlhood dreams made her seem younger, more like his age, more like an equal.

"At least you got the fur coat," he said.

Her hands dropped to her lap, and she wrinkled her nose. "That's about all I got, which is why I didn't leave it for Brandt to take back to the store and get him a refund. It's only half-paid for, anyhow."

The waitress brought the coffee, and Ozzy stared at

her wondering how Maysie could tell she thought he was a stud. It bothered him. Not that some Texas waitress thought he was a sexual athlete—he planned on being a sexual athlete in Paris, anyway—but that he didn't pick up on it. He didn't like people thinking things about him that he didn't know they were thinking.

Maysie emptied three packets of Sweet 'n Low into her cup and then poured cream from a tiny metal container. She raised the cup to her lips with both hands, as if she were taking communion. The steam rose in front of her face, softening her features and making her pretty in the way he'd first seen her in the Wichita terminal. A patch of sunlight sat on her shoulder, turning the steam silver as it drifted away. She took a sip and closed her eyes. "Ah, that's good."

Ozzy sipped his own coffee, but it was bitter and so hot it burned his lips. Maysie put down her cup and leaned across the table. "So, Ozzy, where'y'all from, anyway?"

"Colorado."

"That's a nice state."

"It's okay." He was going to be mysterious. It would be part of his writer's persona, along with his black clothes and artistic sensitivities. Like Edmond Dantès in *The Count of Monte Cristo,* the man without a past. But Maysie would know there was something special about him, this black presence sitting across from her, dark eyes boring into hers, stripping her down to her elemental motivations, laying her soul bare before his writer's mind. Someday she'd see his photograph on the dustcover of a best-seller and gasp, "My God! That's him, the man I met in the bus station. I just—I don't believe it, I just don't believe it!"

Maysie cocked her head to one side. "Don't you like Colorado?"

"Let's just say Colorado doesn't like me."

"What do you mean?"

"Let's just say I had to leave for my health."

"You got asthma or something?"

"No, no, I don't mean my *physical* health. You know what I mean?" She stared at him blankly. "I mean, I had to leave town quickly."

She shrugged. "I figured that much from the coat you're wearing."

"The coat?"

"It's only about three sizes too big for you. A person would have to be deaf, dumb, and blind not to know it wasn't yours. You didn't steal it, did you?"

Ozzy was disappointed. Was that what she thought, that he looked like a thief? "A friend loaned it to me. Gary Grafton. I'm sending it back as soon as we reach New Orleans."

Maysie nodded, but it was more an "I heard you" nod than an "I believe you" nod. She said, "So where'd you get all this money to go to Paris, France?"

"I earned it last summer. My mom has—" He was about to tell Maysie about helping Mom with her tours last summer. He'd done scheduling and written letters and researched her whole China trip, and Mom had paid him five dollars an hour. But Mom was dead, and here he was talking about her as if she were alive. Maysie raised an eyebrow, waiting for him to continue.

"Never mind." Ozzy let his eyes flick around the

room as if he were checking for police. "The less you know, the better."

Maysie shook her finger at him. "It's a good thing I got an eye for faces. Otherwise, I wouldn't trust you for one second."

He gave her a pirate's smile as the waitress brought breakfast. The omelet was so large, it took up one whole plate; the three biscuits were on another. The biscuits were the size of doughnuts and looked like they were covered with gravy. Ozzy dipped a finger and tasted to make sure. Maysie smiled. "Y'all want to borrow my fork?"

"It's gravy."

"What'd you expect?"

He expected plain biscuits with maybe butter or jelly, but it didn't matter. The gravy tasted fine, even if it was more like eating dinner that way.

Ozzy asked Maysie about her family, and she settled back and told him about her father. He was a drifter who couldn't stay three months on a job without hearing about some other, better job somewhere. "Always looking for greener pastures," she said. Her father had worked on Texas oil rigs and Louisiana shrimp boats and Mississippi river barges and Alabama used-car lots and Florida construction crews. It was the construction crew that killed him. He'd gone to work building Disney World, down in Orlando, when a load of reinforcing rods had slipped from a crane. Her father had been underneath holding one of the tag lines. Maysie's face softened as she spoke of him, and a distant look came to her eye.

"He was a little crazy, I guess, but I sure loved him."

Ozzy felt tears spring to his eyes. "I'm sorry, Maysie."

Hearing his voice catch, she gave him a curious look. "Hey, you okay?"

Ozzy rubbed his eye. "My contact lens. Sometimes it gives me trouble." He was embarrassed at the way sadness could sneak up on him and make him feel like a baby. "How big is your family?"

"It's a Texas-size family. I got me four brothers and three sisters."

"Really?"

"I was number three with two brothers above me, so it wasn't the most ideal position to be in. That's probably how come I got married as soon as I got the chance."

Ozzy went back to the omelet and biscuits. "It must be hard to keep track of everybody's names and birthdays and everything."

"Daddy made up a rhyme about it. He changed it every time somebody else was born, but it ended up like this." She made a picture frame with her fingers, peered out, and recited: " 'Darrel was first, then quick came Earl; Maysie was lazy'—that's on account of I was two weeks late being born—'Maysie was lazy, and Pam was a girl; Lynne was a fine one, followed by Brian, then Sandy and Sonny once Momma quit tryin'.' " She grinned and dropped her hands to her lap.

Ozzy was captivated. It wasn't just the way she did it, bouncing her head and almost singing the words, but the whole idea of her father making up rhymes.

"He sounds like fun."

"Oh, he was. Not that he was around that much, but when he was, we had us a ball."

The waitress came to see if they wanted anything else and left the bill. Maysie took a red leather wallet from her purse and began searching for coins.

"That's okay," Ozzy said. "I've got it."

"No, here." She shoved sixty cents across the table. "There's fifty cents for coffee and a dime tip."

They left Jimbo's and walked toward the Kennedy Memorial. Dallas seemed a lot like Denver, with business-type guys in suits and working-type guys in jeans and lawyer-type women in tailored skirts. The only difference was that a lot of the men wore big cowboy hats, just like on the TV show *Dallas.* He half-expected to feel a tap on his shoulder and turn around to find J. R. Ewing giving him an icy smile. "I like that coat you're wearing, Ozzy. I'm going to take control of that coat and I'd advise you not to try and stop me."

It turned out the place Kennedy was shot was really a couple of blocks from the memorial, near a patch of grass called Delaney Plaza. A bunch of people were taking photographs, and a woman was sitting on a bench dabbing her eyes with a handkerchief while her husband stood beside her, looking around and saying in this hypnotized voice, "This is the place, this is the place."

"I don't know what's the big deal," Ozzy muttered. "It's not like he was Abraham Lincoln or something."

"Don't you feel it?" Maysie said in a hushed voice. "This is where history was made."

A man with scraggly blond hair down to his shoulders was wandering from one group to another. He wore a buckskin jacket and pants with leather fringe along the seams. A plastic box hung from his neck by a beaded Indian strap. It was about the size of a shoe box, and on the front, painted in pink nail polish, it said Souvenirs.

"Assassination lizards," he called in a high metallic voice. "Living memorial to a dead memorial, got 'em right here." The man held up a chameleon. "How about it, folks? Living souvenir of the great Dallas tragedy, one dollar."

The chameleon was sandwiched between the man's thumb and fingers, its tiny claws facing outward as if searching for something to hang on to. It turned its head to one side and looked at Ozzy with a single unblinking eye. The chameleon's stomach was the color of the moon, but the rest of its body was an iridescent rainbow that made the buckskin man's dirty hands and cracked fingernails look gross by comparison. There was a thin, black fish line tied around the chameleon's neck like a collar. At the other end of the line an oversize safety pin dangled and danced in the air as the man approached.

Maysie would have kept walking, but Ozzy stopped. "You're really selling a chameleon?"

The buckskin man instantly veered over to him. "Assassination lizard, born and bred in the book depository, the same place L.H.O. shot the P.K. Ka-zowie, nineteen sixty-three. This little scoundrel probably watched him do it, a piece of living history, and I offer him to you for only one dollar, special weekday rate."

The man thrust the lizard at him and grinned. He wasn't the cleanest guy in the world. His breath smelled like a combination of sulfur and stale whiskey, his teeth were crusty and brown, and the shoulders of his jacket were dark and shiny from where his hair brushed against it. Ozzy backed off. "No, no, that's okay."

"Wait a minute." The buckskin man plopped the chameleon down on top of the plastic box. The lid was painted in squares of four separate colors: red, yellow, blue, and white. The chameleon crouched on the blue square without moving.

"See him do his trick," the buckskin man continued. "Changes colors, just like you-know-who in the book depository. Hide out, blend in, lay low, then watch out! Here comes the motorcade. Zap, got a mosquito. Zap, got a fly. That's how they eat, little assassination lizards." The guy glanced at the chameleon and frowned. "Come on, you little suck-heel, do your trick."

He started flicking the chameleon with his finger. Ozzy thought it would run off, but maybe it knew there was a string around its neck, because all it did was crouch lower and try to pull its head into its shoulders.

"Come on, come on." The guy kept flicking it, banging the chameleon's head on the blue square.

"Quit that," Maysie said. "We ain't buying it, so leave it alone."

"Ah, he's been spiteful all day, haven't you, you little monster?" The guy flicked the chameleon again, and Maysie reached over and grabbed his arm.

"Cut it out, I said."

He looked as if he were seeing her for the first time. A slow grin spread across his face, and Maysie let go quickly.

"It's my lizard, lady."

"That don't give you the right to hurt it."

"You want to buy him?"

"No, I told you." She turned to Ozzy and grabbed his arm. "Come on."

They started back to the terminal, but the buckskin man followed them.

"Well, now," he said in a loud voice. "I guess he's my little old assassination lizard and I can do anything I want with him. I can hit him or toss him under a truck or use him as fish bait—"

Ozzy was going to ignore the guy, but Maysie stopped and whirled around.

"You do and I'll whup you up alongside the head so bad you'll be seeing stars at noon the rest of your life."

The buckskin man lifted the chameleon off the ground by the string and said, "Or, if I don't have enough money for dinner, maybe I'll just eat him."

"Oh my God!" Maysie grabbed Ozzy's arm so quickly he thought she was having a heart attack. "He's a geek. He's a geek, Ozzy."

"A what?"

"A geek. One of them perverts that eats the heads off chickens and gobbles lizards. I seen one in Biloxi, made me sick to my stomach."

"Yum, yum." The buckskin man licked his lips and bounced the chameleon up and down.

"He'll eat him, he'll eat that creature."

"Don't worry," Ozzy said calmly. "He's not going to eat it."

The buckskin man leaned toward them and whispered, "Just watch." He tilted his head back and opened his mouth.

"Oh, Ozzy, Ozzy!"

Maysie's fingers clamped into his arm, and Ozzy bought the chameleon. On the way back to the bus he tried to give it to her, but she didn't want it.

"I just didn't want that geek to eat him," she said. "You better let him go."

"Here? In the middle of downtown?"

"Give it to somebody, then. Do something with it."

Ozzy glanced at the chameleon, which was riding on his shoulder. "Hey, look what he did."

"He crap on your jacket?"

"No, look what color he is. Red like the jacket. He's matching me."

She opened her mouth to say something and then noticed the clock on a bank building.

"Oh my God, we're going to miss that bus."

They ran the rest of the way and caught the bus just as it was backing out of the parking stall. They sat down, breathless and laughing, and laughed even more when they realized that the chameleon was still on Ozzy's shoulder.

Chapter 12

BRANDT WASN'T HER FIRST HUSBAND. Her first husband was named Leon, and Maysie told Ozzy about him on the way to Houston.

"He was down for Mardi Gras, and I was hanging around Pat O'Brien's, looking for fun and Mister Right. Leon, he was from Memphis, and I fell for him on account of his curly blond hair and big crooked smile . . ." She made a face. "I don't know. I was young and stupid."

Maysie was putting on nail polish as she talked. Ozzy noticed she liked wearing a lot of makeup around her eyes and on her fingernails. She put on the nail polish the same way she did the mascara, with quick, short strokes. The smell of it was like ice in his nose and reminded him of model-car glue.

"Anyhow," she continued. "We had us a hot little romance, but I was smart enough to save something for dessert. I held out until we was married. Like to drove him crazy, trying to get me drunk enough to go all the way and me never losing sense of where we were and what was going on. He said he owned a garage up in Memphis, and on the last night of the carnival we got drunk and married and honeymooned all in one night. One morning I was Miss Maysie Fontaine and the next morning I woke up Mrs. Leon Fuchs."

"Fontaine? Is that French?"

"Who knows? Maybe a hundred years ago it was." She waved her hand gently to dry the fingernails.

The chameleon ran partway down Ozzy's arm and stopped. "Whoa, where are you going, little guy?"

"You'd best tie that thing to your shirt, or he'll get away, sure."

Ozzy hated to chain the chameleon, but Maysie was right. It would be lousy if somebody stepped on him or he got stuck in a heating vent. He tied the free end of the string through a buttonhole and returned the conversation to Leon. He wanted to know more about their wild honeymoon, but Maysie was done with that part. It turned out Leon didn't own a garage, he only worked in one. And he lived with his crippled father, who kept feeling Maysie up whenever Leon was at work. Eventually they got their own apartment, but it didn't help much, because Leon would get drunk and hit her.

"He was always sorry in the morning," Maysie said. "Lie his head on my lap and promise never to do it again. Fight, beat up, make up—that was the way of it. I kept thinking maybe it was my fault. Something I done or didn't do that made him act that way. I even canceled out on seeing Momma one Christmas on account of I didn't want her to see my bruises. But nothing helped, and one day Leon hauled off and broke my nose with a coffeepot and that was the end of it. I was gone."

"He broke your nose?"

"See that little ridge?" She leaned toward him and pointed awkwardly, keeping her fingers spread so that the polish wouldn't smear. Ozzy couldn't imagine anybody hitting Maysie. The thought made him sick.

"Is that why you left this time?"

"Left where? Left Brandt?"

"Did he hit you?"

"You crazy, Ozzy? Brandt wouldn't touch a hair on my head. He loves me."

She said it with such force and conviction, he was taken aback. "Then why'd you leave?"

"I told you that."

"You mean because you had an argument about where to live?"

"It's more than that. I want me a family and a house and friends and I want them all in one place. I want to be part of somewhere. I want to be able to walk down the street in fifty years and say to myself, 'Yeah, that's where the old bank used to be' and 'That's Mr. So-and-so's drugstore, where we charged up medicine that time the kids got sick.' And I want to visit a neighbor who can say, 'Lord, yes, Maysie, I remember that little boy of yours when he fell into the river hunting tadpoles and I had to . . .' " She slowed to a stop and shook her head. "Whatever. You know what I mean."

Ozzy knew. She didn't want to be an outsider. He was going to ask her why Brandt didn't want to live in one place, but he felt a bug on his neck and flicked it off without looking. The chameleon bounced off the window and landed in his lap.

"Oh no."

For a second Ozzy was afraid he'd killed it, but when he touched it, the chameleon ran across his chest and under his arm as far as the string would let it.

"I'm sorry, boy. I didn't mean it."

Maysie twisted the cap tight on the nail polish and stuffed it back in her purse. "How can you tell it's a *he*? You know how to read the sex on them things?"

"No, I don't know. He seems like a he, though."

"So you're going to call him Sammy instead of Rosie, huh?"

Ozzy looked at the chameleon. It was like having a piece of rainbow on his arm. "No, not Sammy. He's got to have the right kind of name."

"How about Butch? We had a dog named Butch once."

"Scintilla." The word drifted into his mind like a feather. "That's what his name should be. Scintilla."

"Sin-what?"

"Scintilla. It means a little bit of something. But it's also a thin word, thin and fast, like he is."

"A thin word? What do you mean a 'thin' word?"

"The way it comes into your mouth. It feels thin, you know?"

Maysie wrinkled her nose. "Words don't feel, they mean. They mean whatever they say. *Thin* is *thin* and *scin—scintilla,* or whatever it is, that's just long and means what you said. A little bit of something. So call him Bitty or Tiny or Pee-wee if that's what you want."

Ozzy shook his head. There were right words and

wrong words, and it didn't have to do with what they meant. Some words were like sipping ginger ale and some were like chewing a meatball and some were like biting into a toasted muffin, but the way they felt was different from how they tasted. It was hard to explain, so he just said, "No, he doesn't seem like any of those words. He seems like Scintilla."

"Call him Tilla, then. Scin-tilla is too long a word for a creature that puny."

"He's a chameleon, Maysie. That's how come he's so pretty."

"Pretty or no, he eats flies and mosquitoes, same as the rest of them."

THE NEXT REST STOP was a motel, café, and gas station called God's Little Acre. Ozzy couldn't see any reason for its being there except that it was halfway between Dallas and Houston. The motel and café were part of the same building, which was in a U-shape with some playground equipment in the middle. The gas station was on the north side of the motel, and a fenced area that was the actual God's Little Acre was on the south. A big sign over the gate to the fenced area said Walk Through the Living Bible. Your Favorite Scenes Beautifully Re-created. Educational and Inspirational.

They went over and looked through the cyclone fence. God's Little Acre was like a miniature golf course, except that there were little plaster statues instead of windmills and anthills. The statues were about two feet high and grouped into different scenes from the Bible. Each scene had a number, and in the center

God stood three feet high, dressed in robes and reaching his arms out to bless everything.

"That's cute," Maysie said. She pointed to scene number sixteen. "Look, that's Jesus getting baptized."

Ozzy didn't think it was cute. He thought it was pretty stupid, really. If God was going to put a Little Acre anywhere, it wouldn't be in Texas. He left Maysie and went behind the café to find a box for Tilla. There were a lot of big, one-gallon cans coated with tomato paste or mayonnaise, and soggy boxes full of wilted lettuce, apple cores, and chicken gizzards. It wasn't the most appetizing thing to be doing, digging through garbage with a chameleon on your shoulder and a giant fan in the side of the wall blowing kitchen fumes in your face. He was about to give up when he spotted an empty Kleenex box. It had a big oval opening, but that wouldn't matter, because he could attach the string to the box so that Tilla couldn't get away. He took the box and put some dirt and grass in the bottom, along with a chunk of wood so that there'd be something to climb on.

Maysie was doing exercises in front of the café. A milk truck was in the parking lot beside her. Its tank was a flattened metal cylinder, an oval, so that everything reflected in it looked squashed and fat. Maysie stood with her feet spread, twisting back and forth with her hands on her hips. Her reflection looked like one of the God's Little Acre statues come to life. A blue station wagon drove through the parking lot, its tires scrunching on the gravel. Ozzy watched its reflection grow longer and longer, stretching like blue taffy, until all of a sudden the trunk snapped forward and caught up with the rest of the car.

"Look." Ozzy pointed to the world reflected in the milk truck. "Look how weird it looks."

She stared at the container and waved. "It's like a funhouse mirror, except I like the ones that make you look thin better."

Ozzy put the Kleenex box on the ground and got out his notepad. He flipped it open and made a new heading: "Descriptions."

"What're you doing?"

"I'm writing down what it looks like." He thought for a minute, then wrote, "Milk truck—like a Thermos bottle on wheels."

"Girl does what?" Maysie said in a puzzled voice. She leaned closer, staring at the notepad. "What is that thing?"

"It's my literary notebook. Where I write down things to use in famous writing."

He started to put the notebook back in his pocket, but Maysie reached over and took it. " 'Girl sleeps with mouth open,' " she read. She looked up with a frown. "What does that mean?"

"It was cute, you know, last night when you were sleeping—"

"This is me?"

Ozzy smiled and gave a little shrug. He figured she'd be pleased, flattered to think he was saving her a place in his famous writing. Instead her frown deepened as she read on.

" 'Girl snores'!" When she looked up this time, there

was no doubt that she wasn't flattered. "You're going to write that I snore?"

"No, it says *'girls* snore,' plural. I never knew they did."

Her mouth clamped shut, and Ozzy knew he was in trouble. "Uh, we better go back to the bus—" he began, but it was too late.

" 'Jaygool—Low-Class Phrases'!" She snapped the notepad against her knee and glared at him. "Is that what you think? I'm low-class?"

"I didn't mean it that way," he said helplessly. He reached for the notepad, but she drew back.

"Just how *did* you mean it, Ozzy? Writing down all how I talk so you can make me out some low-class, ignorant trash in some book, just how did you mean it?"

"It's not that, Maysie. It's just material. They all do it."

"Who all does it?"

"Famous writers. That's how they—"

"Not to *me* they don't. I'm nobody's material but my own. And if I *was* material, it wouldn't be low-class, ignorant trash material."

"Here, come on." He reached again for the notepad, but she stayed away.

"No wonder you been so nice, loaning me money, asking questions all about me and my family. You've been collecting me up to put me in a book."

"That's not it."

"What else you got in here?" She started to read, and Ozzy moved forward.

"You stay back!" Maysie yelled. A young couple in

matching maroon sweaters paused to watch from the door of the café. Ozzy cringed. "Maysie, just . . . let me have it, okay?"

"You want it?" She looked around and spotted a metal trash can. "You can have it. You just come dig it out of the trash, because that's where it belongs."

"Don't—"

She threw the notepad into the trash, turned, and yelled, "Come dig it out if you want it, but let me tell you something, Ozzy Mills. I'm nobody's guinea pig, and that was a rotten thing you done, so you just stay clear of me until we get to New Orleans and I get my double-diamond ring back and be done with you."

The family from the station wagon scattered like pigeons as she stomped past them on her way to the bus. They looked after her, then turned to stare at Ozzy. He gave a weak smile and a little shrug to show that he was as baffled as they were. They went into the café, the father guarding the rear with occasional glances over his shoulder at Ozzy. The door closed, and he was alone with a chameleon in God's Little Acre.

Chapter 13

MAYSIE sat beside someone else on the bus, a gray-haired lady two seats back from the door. When Ozzy got on, Maysie was talking up a storm with her.

"Really? It was Tom Selleck in person?"

"At the very next table," the lady said. "That's where Bunny saw him."

"Well, I hope you're going right out and visit, because that's just what I'd do if I had a daughter living in Hollywood."

She made a point of ignoring him, so Ozzy ignored her back. He wasn't going to betray his artistic destiny just because some girl who was running away from her husband didn't understand how famous writing worked. What was she so upset about, anyway? It wasn't like he'd tricked her or ripped her off or anything. He wished he had *Famous Authorship* with him. He could have shown Maysie the chapter on Sources. He could have proved it was an ancient, honorable tradition, using people and places from real life as models for fiction.

The bus moved back onto the freeway, and Ozzy put Tilla in the Kleenex box. "We don't care, do we, boy?" He pushed the safety pin through the cardboard and snapped it shut. The chameleon seemed happy enough. Tilla was easy to get along with, not like *some* people. "We don't care what she does."

Ozzy brought out the notebook he'd retrieved from the trash, flipped it open to the expense record, and wrote, "Breakfast = $3.50; Tilla = $1.00." He added it up. The expenses came to $98.65, which left $50.35 to get to Paris. He'd have to be careful in New Orleans. He'd have to stay someplace cheap, like the YMCA, and get the first ship he could find. Maybe he'd be lucky and find one tomorrow so that he could be on the Left Bank by Christmas.

He put away the notepad and looked out the window so that he wouldn't think about Maysie. There wasn't anything to see except the low, rolling plains, a sky that was turning slowly overcast, and an endless highway. That was the trouble with Texas, it was so big, it turned your thoughts back on you so that you couldn't get away from your own mind. Ozzy started remembering things, like what Maysie said about being a guinea pig and how Gary was always treating life like a fruit-fly experiment. Then he remembered something he hadn't thought about in a long time. It was one of the few times Dad had ever gotten really mad at Lance. It was back when Lance was a sophomore in high school and was taking pictures for the school paper, *The Eagle.* His sophomore year was Lance's photographer phase, and he carried this Minolta camera everywhere he went. One weekend Dad took Ozzy and Lance to a Broncos game, and when they were coming back from Denver, there had been an accident. Two cars had smashed up, and the ambulance hadn't gotten there yet, so there was this guy wandering around holding a cloth against his head and a woman lying on the ground while people bandaged her bloody leg. Dad slowed down, and Lance stuck his Minolta against the window and began taking pictures.

Dad said, "Don't do that."

"It's a real accident!" He kept taking pictures, and Dad reached over and grabbed his arm. "I said stop it."

"Dad!"

"Put down the camera."

"It's a scoop, Dad. Maybe I can sell them to the *Post* and win a scholarship." He brought the camera to his eye again, and Dad almost swerved off the road when he lunged across the seat and yanked the camera away. Lance was furious. "You almost broke my camera!"

"Forget the camera, think about those people. It's not television just because you have a camera in front of your face."

"It's news and we were right here for it. You just wrecked everything, Dad. Thanks a lot."

"How would you like it if you were hurt and bleeding and someone came up and stuck a camera in your face?"

"I wasn't sticking it in anybody's face."

"You know what I mean."

"If Mom were here, she'd let me take pictures."

Dad paused and then said in a low voice, "No, she'd feel the same way."

"Yeah, Lance," Ozzy said. "She'd feel the same way."

"You shut up! Nobody asked you."

Remembering it now, Ozzy couldn't help thinking that writing down what Maysie said was a little like Lance trying to take pictures of bloody accident victims. He took out the notepad and opened it to the "Low-class Phrases" page. He crossed out the heading and wrote, "Southern Phrases." Then he got up and went to the front of the bus to show Maysie.

The old lady was still talking a mile a minute, but when Ozzy stopped beside her, she paused and looked up.

"Excuse me," Ozzy said. He turned to Maysie and held up the notepad. "I just wanted to show you—I changed the heading, see?"

Maysie turned to the old lady. "Do you know this boy?"

"No, I don't."

"Come on, Maysie, I'm sorry, okay? Give me a break."

"You must have the wrong person," the old lady said. "Her name is Judy, not Maysie."

Ozzy stared at the old lady and then at Maysie. She gave him a smug smile and said, "Judy McNamara."

"Oh, come on . . ."

Maysie turned back to the old lady. "I know just what you mean about sciatica. My grandma had it, and for the longest time the doctors thought it was some awful thing like muscular dystrophy, but then she went to this special clinic in Mobile . . ."

She kept chatting, and Ozzy went back to his seat. He wondered who she was, Maysie Perlmutter or Judy McNamara? Had she been telling him stories all along? Then he remembered her smug smile and the way she'd made up stuff when that guy sat beside her in Wichita, and he knew. She was Maysie Perlmutter, all right, but she wasn't going to talk to him.

His mind returned to the incident of Lance trying to take pictures. Something else bothered him. He wasn't so sure Mom would have told Lance to put down the camera. She might have encouraged him to take photographs the same way she encouraged Ozzy to keep a notebook. Thinking this made him feel like he was betraying Mom, so he pushed the thought aside and spent the rest of the way to Houston trying to catch a fly against the window for Tilla.

THE HOUSTON TERMINAL was a long, low building with a lot of people waiting for buses and the usual number of bag ladies and bums hanging around. Ozzy wondered where all the homeless people came from and why they liked big cities instead of small towns. If he ever became a bum, he'd move to a small town like Capitol, where people would get to know him and maybe give him a quarter for sweeping the sidewalk or something. He sure wouldn't go to a bus station in a big city, where strangers ignored you and drug perverts strangled you in your sleep.

When Maysie got off the bus, he followed her into the terminal. Carrying Tilla in the Kleenex box, he pretended he was a CIA agent and she was a Russian spy on her way to deliver a secret code hidden in a tube of toothpaste. He expected her to go to a restaurant, but instead she went to a newsstand and picked up a copy of *Screen Romances.* Ozzy hid behind a column and watched. Maysie just stood there reading, and Ozzy could see the sleazy guys in coffee-stained trench coats reading *Playboy* and *Hustler* right beside her looking her over. Even the bald guy at the cash register. He wore a frayed Hawaiian shirt and chewed a plastic yellow cigarette holder with a brown cigarette stuck in it. He leaned across the counter and ran his eyes all over Maysie, wiggling the cigarette holder while he did it. Maysie didn't notice, but it made Ozzy sick. He felt like going over and stuffing the guy's cigarette down his throat.

He wished Maysie would go to the restaurant, but it looked like she was going to spend the hour in Houston right there at Zephyr News and Candies. He went outside and looked around. Two blocks up the street there was a Ramada Inn. Ozzy jogged to the Ramada Inn and got a book of matches from the desk clerk. When he got back to the terminal, Maysie was still reading. He came up beside her. "Hi."

She ignored him.

"Look, Maysie, I'm sorry about writing stuff down. I won't do it anymore, okay?"

"Doesn't matter. I ain't going to talk to you no more, anyway."

Ozzy had already figured that out, so he had prepared a dramatic gesture. He put the Kleenex box with Tilla on the floor, took out the notepad, and ripped out the two pages with stuff about Maysie on them.

"Look, I want to show you something."

He lit a match and held the two pieces of paper over the flame. "See? This is the stuff I wrote. See what I'm doing?"

"Ozzy, stop." She grabbed at his hand as the flames began to take hold. He swung his arm away so she wouldn't get burned. A man behind them jumped back, bumping a book stand.

"Don't," Ozzy said to Maysie. "I'm just—"

The sleazy guy at the cash register let out a yell and came over the counter like he had springs on his shoes.

"You friggin' crazy kid!"

The guy looked like he was going to hit him. Ozzy dropped the paper and put up his hands. Instantly the guy began stomping on the paper, still cussing him out.

"Don't hit the box," Ozzy yelled. He grabbed the Kleenex box and handed it to Maysie. "Here, hold Tilla."

Maysie pulled him away. "Come on, let's go."

The fire was out, and the sleazy guy turned on them. His eyes were bulging like Ping-Pong balls, and his face was all red and pulsating.

"You friggin' pyromaniac, what're you trying to do? Burn me out?"

"It was only a piece of paper."

"Only a piece of paper!" The guy's fingers were twitching like worms. "Did Manny send you, is that it?"

People were gathering, and someone said, "What happened?"

"Friggin' kid tried to burn my place down."

Maysie was still pulling him toward the door. She

called back, "It was an accident. He was trying to light a cigarette."

"A cigarette!" the sleazy guy bellowed. "I got books here. I got magazines, newspapers, the stuff's like gunpowder . . ."

Maysie pulled him out the door, and Ozzy realized he wasn't going to get hit. He felt a strange elation. He'd gotten away with it. He'd looked tough. Maysie must be impressed.

"The guy was afraid to hit me, did you see?"

"Here. Take your lizard."

"Did you see the way he came over the counter? Unbelievable."

"You could have got us locked up."

"For what? We didn't do anything."

"You started a fire, that's what." She stood there with her arms crossed, looking around the street like she was trying to figure out what to do.

"Listen, Maysie, I'm sorry about what I wrote down about you. It's not like you thought, but it doesn't matter—I won't write anything more. I won't even remember it if you don't want, honest."

She looked at him and shook her head. "Sometimes I feel like catnip to crazies. How come I had to meet up with somebody like you?"

They went to a McDonald's on the corner, and Ozzy ordered a Big Mac, fries, and a chocolate shake. Maysie asked for coffee.

"Is that all you eat?" Ozzy asked. "Coffee?"

"I'll eat when I get home."

"Yeah, but we don't get there until after midnight."

She shrugged, and he suddenly realized she had no

money. He offered to lend her some, but she shook her head. "I already took enough off you."

"So? You can pay me back."

"I only owe what I have to."

Ozzy doubled his order, and when Maysie protested, he said, "I'm super-hungry." When they sat down at a booth, he pushed the second order across to her. She frowned.

"Ozzy, I told you . . ."

"Throw it away, then, because I'm not eating it."

It was different between them now. It felt more equal, more comfortable. Now that he wasn't using her for his famous writing, Maysie became more like a whole person where before she'd been a cute face and neat body and odd habits and unfamiliar words and bits and pieces of description.

He told her about Mom. He did it without thinking or planning what kind of effect it would have on her, he just told her. He explained how the family had driven up to the mountains to get a tree and how Dad had let Mom go get the car even though the road was dangerous and he knew she was a terrible driver. He told her about the argument over Mom's last wishes and how he'd accused Dad of letting the accident happen.

Maysie sat and listened, her eyes locked on his, her hand moving across the table to touch his arm. When he finished, she closed her eyes and whispered, "Oh, Ozzy, whatever have you done?"

"Me? It's not me, it's him."

She opened her eyes and looked at him sadly. "You really think it was your daddy's fault?"

"Yes!" The quickness of his response surprised them

both. "Maybe not totally," he added. "But he knew about Mom's driving."

"She knew how to drive, though."

"You don't understand, Maysie. She was different. She didn't do things in the average, mindless way. Dad knew it. Everybody knew it. Like if there's a parking place on the other side of the street, she'll just turn into it, while Dad goes around the block sixteen thousand times and loses out. I don't mean if cars are coming, but she's got this thing about wasting time on trivia and . . ."

He hesitated, aware that he was talking about Mom in the present tense, aware that the more he talked, the more confused he got. "Things like that," he finished lamely.

Maysie shook her head. "Your daddy must be worried sick."

"I don't care."

"Yes, you do. You better call that poor man."

He drew back. "It's his fault, Maysie. I'm never going to talk to him again."

It had been a mistake to tell her. Maysie's image blurred and faded into the jumble of the room. He felt a kind of panic come over him. It was the same panic as when he was a kid, playing in a vacant lot with some neighborhood boys and they'd found a corroded car battery. Ozzy rubbed his eyes after touching it, and they began to burn. One of the other kids told him that he had sixty seconds to rinse his eyes or go blind forever. He remembered running to the nearest house, frantic and crying, and how the lady who came to the front door didn't understand that he needed to use her sink. The other kid had been fooling around, but Ozzy was eight, and to him it was real. He remembered the fear and hysteria that pulled him like quicksand, standing there on the front porch, knowing his eyesight was slipping away. That was the feeling growing in him now, that same sense of inescapable catastrophe.

"Hey, hey." Maysie shook his arm gently. "Are you all right?"

Her face came back into focus, brow furrowed and green eyes dark with concern.

"I'm not calling." The words burst out of him. He was breathing in short, shallow gulps.

"All right, it's all right, Ozzy. I ain't going to twist your arm to make you do it."

"I can't, Maysie. Don't you see?"

"All right, don't. But just relax now, you're all worked up."

She kept talking, and the panic drained away. Ozzy didn't know whether she understood or not. He didn't know if he understood, but he knew he couldn't talk to Dad. Not now. Not until he reached Paris and wrote the book that would make everything the way it was supposed to be.

On the way back to the bus Maysie said, "So where are you staying in New Orleans?"

"I don't know. I guess the YMCA."

"You don't know a single soul?" She shook his head. "All right, then, I'm going to make me a phone call."

She veered toward a telephone booth, but Ozzy grabbed her arm. "Who are you calling?"

"I'm going to call Momma, see if you can stay with us."

"You're not going to call my dad, are you?

"Call your daddy? No, that's for you to decide. But I don't want you staying alone in New Orleans, hear?"

He let go of her arm and stood watching people on the street while Maysie called. A man holding hands with a little boy leaned low so that he could hear what the boy was saying. The boy's eyes sparkled, and every now and then he did a little skip. Ozzy looked after them as they moved down the sidewalk at the child's pace, the other pedestrians weaving quickly around them. For the first time in his life he wished he were younger instead of older.

Maysie came up to him. "It's all set. I just hope you don't mind sleeping on the porch."

"No, that's fine."

They turned back to the terminal. At the end of the block the man and the little boy turned the corner and disappeared. The little boy was riding on the man's shoulders now, and Ozzy would have given anything in the world to be riding up there with him.

Chapter 14

THEY TALKED A LOT on the way to New Orleans, and Maysie told him what happened with Brandt. "I was real careful the second time around," she said. "I told Brandt right off I wasn't going to bring up my kids like gypsies, dragging around after their daddy like I done. So he says, 'When do you figure on having kids?' And I told him, 'It doesn't matter as long as they stay put in a single house and a single school.' So Brandt, he agrees to work the towers for two years and then transfer over to the fabrication plant in Mobile so we can settle in. After a year we had us seven thousand dollars tucked away, and he starts talking about getting a new truck. 'With what money?' I ask. 'Now, babe, don't be like that.' " She paused and looked past him. "Is that rain?"

Ozzy looked outside. It was more of a mist than a rain. The headlights of oncoming cars were white cones, and the pavement glistened darkly.

"Anyway," Maysie continued, "the long and the

short of it was that he got the truck and I took off, with a couple of details in between."

It was cozy sitting beside her with the rain outside and the heat curling up around their legs. The time passed quickly, and when they reached New Orleans, Ozzy was surprised to discover it was two-thirty in the morning.

Maysie's mom was waiting at the station. Ozzy thought that after having eight kids, she might look old and bent. Instead she reminded him of a soldier cut from cardboard, standing tall and flat with a yellow raincoat draped over her shoulders like a cape. As soon as she saw her, Maysie ran forward, and the two embraced. Mrs. Fontaine had black hair with a lot of gray and was an inch or so taller than Maysie. When he got close, Ozzy could see that his impression of her as a soldier was wrong. She had soft hazel eyes and stared over Maysie's shoulder with an expression more like a worried nurse than an army general.

Maysie pulled back, still holding her mom's arms. "Did he call, Momma?"

Mrs. Fontaine pursed her lips and shook her head. "No, honey, he ain't called."

They stared at each other a long moment. Then Maysie remembered Ozzy and turned to introduce him. "This is the man I told you about."

Mrs. Fontaine dipped her head in kind of a cross between a nod and a bow. "We're much obliged to you for your help, Mr. Mills."

"That's okay," Ozzy mumbled. Hearing himself called mister with a Southern accent reminded him of the sheriff in all the Sidney Poitier movies. It also reminded him that his hair was greasy and he hadn't had a bath in two days.

Mrs. Fontaine let out a little sigh. "Well, let's get your bags and get on out of here. You must be bone-tired, the both of you."

"This is it, Momma." Maysie swung her fishnet bag. "This is all I brought."

"Oh, honey."

"And Ozzy there, his worldly possessions are in that shoebox. We're regular gypsies here."

It was still raining, and the parking lot was filled with puddles. Maysie's mom had brought an umbrella, but by the time they got to the car, Ozzy's shoes were soaked. Maysie climbed in the backseat. "You sit up front with Momma."

"That's okay, I'll get in back."

"No, Mr. Mills," Mrs. Fontaine called from behind the steering wheel. "You're company, and we always have company ride up front where they can see the sights."

The car was a blue Chevy station wagon about ten years old, but it looked like it had just rolled off the assembly line. The seats were covered with clear plastic, and the rain bounded off the hood as if the car were painted with oil. Maysie leaned forward with her elbows over the front seat, talking to her mom.

It turned out that Mrs. Fontaine lived across the Mississippi River in a town called Avery. As they crossed the bridge, Ozzy got his first look at New Orleans. The downtown lights shone like jewels on black velvet, stopping at the water's edge where the river carved out a dark, inky crescent. What caught his eye were the ships, half a dozen of them, tied along the river's edge. One of them was lit up with spotlights, and he could see a crane lifting a white container and swinging it ashore.

Mrs. Fontaine said, "Have you ever been to New Orleans before, Mr. Mills?"

"No, ma'am, this is my first time."

"Then Maysie will have to show you the sights before you leave." She turned to her daughter. "You can't let Mr. Mills leave without seeing our French Quarter, even if he is on his way to France."

"You can call me Ozzy. It's okay."

"Thank you, Ozzy, I'll just do that. You feel free to call me Cora Mae."

Ozzy didn't say anything. There was no way he was going to call somebody his parents' age Cora Mae. You didn't do that unless you were married or had a college degree.

Ozzy couldn't tell much about Avery except that it was mostly residential and had old-fashioned streetlights hanging from green metal poles. Mrs. Fontaine owned a boardinghouse called Felicity Lodge. It was a three-story house with a wrought-iron fence and circular driveway. Ozzy could tell it must have been a fancy place once because the door had big brass doorknobs and leaded-glass panes. As soon as they stepped inside, a calico cat came dancing out of the living room. Maysie knelt to pick him up.

"Hello, little Lolly cat. Did you miss me?"

Mrs. Fontaine put the umbrella in an engraved metal cylinder, then took Ozzy's parka and hung it on a polished mahogany coatrack behind the door. Facing them was a circular stairway and, to the right, a large archway leading to a living room.

"What we've done is divide the house," Mrs. Fontaine explained. "Our guests have the old living room and dining room as well as the front porch, while the kids and me stay in the back rooms."

Ozzy's room was an enclosed porch with a big television and a fold-out couch that was already made up into a bed. Ozzy could tell that there were kids in the house because there was an Atari unit hooked up to the TV and toys on the shelves. Maysie's mom offered to feed him, but what Ozzy really wanted was a hot shower. Every time he lifted his arm, he felt like the bad guy on a deodorant commercial. Mrs. Fontaine gave him a washcloth and towel and showed him the bathroom. He made it a quick shower so that he wouldn't hog the bathroom and when he got out, he realized he didn't have any clean clothes or even a toothbrush. He would have to buy some stuff tomorrow. He wadded up some toilet paper and rubbed his teeth and then climbed back into the same crusty clothes.

Maysie and her mom were in the living room talking in low tones. Maysie sat on the sofa with her legs tucked beneath her, while Mrs. Fontaine sat beside her, holding her hands. The expression on Maysie's face was tired and sad until Ozzy came in. Then she smiled.

"Feel better?"

"Yeah, that was great."

She gestured to the porch. "I closed the door so Lolly wouldn't get in and mess with Tilla."

"Good idea."

The hot shower had relaxed him and made him

drowsy. He thanked Mrs. Fontaine for her hospitality and went to bed. The slow, steady drumming of the rain on the roof and the low murmur of voices from the living room lulled him instantly to sleep.

HE WOKE UP with the sun in his eyes. For a minute he thought he was dreaming about a greenhouse. The porch had windows on three sides, and outside was a glorious green. Vines framed the windows, and magnolias marked the far corners of the lawn. In the center of the yard was a circular flower garden, built in tiers and topped with a plaster birdbath. The rain had stopped, but everything was wet, and the sun sparkled off a thousand hidden droplets. Ozzy turned on his back and listened to the sounds of the house coming to life—the creaking stairs, doors closing, water running, and the ebb and flow of muffled voices. Two kids were arguing outside his door.

"It's not for the year, Sonny," said a girl's voice. "It's just as long as I say you can have it, okay?"

"No."

"Then give it back."

"It's mine. You gave it to me."

"No, I didn't, I just loaned it. Now, give it back."

"You got a new book bag, and I didn't get anything."

"It doesn't matter—"

Their voices faded as they went into the kitchen. How many kids had Maysie said were still at home? Four? He wondered what time it was. He should get up. Instead he turned on his side and dozed off.

The click of the doorknob turning woke him. The

door opened slowly, toward him, so he couldn't tell who it was. He was going to say something when Maysie's voice called out, "Sonny!" The door shut quickly. "I told you, somebody's sleeping in there."

The same child's voice that he'd heard earlier said, "I want to see the lizard."

"Well, you'll just have to wait. You don't go walking into people's rooms when they're sleeping. What's the matter with you?"

"I want to see it before I go to school."

"I don't care what you want, now, come on."

Ozzy heard them go into the kitchen so he got up quickly and put his clothes on. He wondered if he should fold up the sheets and blanket or just leave them? If he was lucky, he'd get a ship today and not be back. He folded everything and stacked it at one end of the couch, with the pillow on top. Tilla had climbed up on top of the Kleenex box, where he stood like a figurehead, his chest and head thrust high in the air. He looked faintly blue, just like the box.

"You hungry, Tilla?" He unhooked the pin and lifted the chameleon to his shoulder. "We'll have to feed you, huh, boy?"

Ozzy went to the kitchen, and Maysie introduced him to her little sister and brother. Sandy was nine years old, plump, with a round face and short black hair that sat on her head like a knit cap. Sonny was a year younger but a lot smaller. He had a bunched-up little nose that seemed to pull the rest of his face toward it. As soon as he saw Tilla, he came running over.

"Be careful, Sonny," Maysie warned. She was wearing a red-and-white-striped cotton nightgown and hadn't put on any makeup. Seeing her in something different from the jeans and white fur coat was like seeing her again for the first time, and like the first time, his first impression was that she was pretty.

Mrs. Fontaine turned from the stove and said, "I'm cooking up a mess of pancakes, Ozzy, and besides that there's cereal and fresh fruit and orange juice and whatever else you want, just ask for it. Can't be bashful around here when it comes to food."

Sonny was standing on his tiptoes, petting Tilla, his eyes bright with excitement. "Can you put him on my shoulder?"

"No," Maysie called. "You leave him on Ozzy's shoulder so he don't get hurt."

"I won't hurt him."

"Let the poor man sit down, Sonny."

Ozzy untied Tilla and lifted him onto Sonny's shoulder. "Just move slow and don't frighten him."

Sonny was cross-eyed trying to watch the chameleon on his shoulder. An old man appeared in the doorway to the dining room. He wore black pants almost up to his armpits and a Panama hat. As soon as she saw him, Maysie called out in a warning voice, "Good morning, Mr. Porter."

Mrs. Fontaine looked around quickly. "What is it, Mr. Porter?"

The old man's lips quivered. "The orange juice glasses, I don't see them on the table."

"They'll be there, Mr. Porter," Mrs. Fontaine said in a loud voice. "Never you worry."

"I know it's not quite eight o'clock." Mr. Porter held out his arm and tapped a rectangular wristwatch. "But there's no juice glasses or silverware and I thought maybe it was late breakfast today."

"It's not a late breakfast, not today." Mrs. Fontaine looked up at the ceiling and called, "Lynne?" Then she said to Maysie, "Watch this thing for me." She went past Ozzy and disappeared upstairs.

Maysie explained that they served breakfast to the guests between eight and nine and then dinner between five and six. "The family usually eats right before them in the morning and right after in the evening."

"And it's Lynnie's week to set the table," Sandy added.

"Look, Sandy." Sonny pushed his shoulder with the chameleon on it toward his sister. "He likes me and his name is Teela."

"No, it's not," Sandy said primly. "It's Tilla, don't you know nothing?"

"That's right," Maysie said. "It's short for Scintilla, which means something itty-bitty in writer language."

"You're thinking of Teela in *Masters of the Universe,*" Sandy told him in a low voice.

"No I'm *not.*" Sonny touched the chameleon. "Tilla, Tilla, Tilla." He looked at Sandy. "He likes boys better than girls."

Maysie gave him a newspaper. "You can check in here for ships. They got lists of every one coming and going."

At first he thought it was a joke or some kind of racial slur, because the name of the paper, the *Times-Picayune,* looked like some kind of "pickaninny" word. But it turned out the paper was real and had been around for over a hundred years without any riots or protests about the name. He found a list of ships in port under "Marine Log." There were separate columns for arrivals and departures, and he couldn't believe the names of the ships. He expected things like *Flying Cloud* and *Annabel Lee,* but half the ships had foreign names like *Kyriaki* and *Genista* and the other half had business names like *Sealand Economy* and *Exxon Baton Rouge.* The only halfway romantic one was a Lykes ship, which had a woman's name. *Almeria Lykes* sounded like it might even be a European ship. It was berthed at the Poydras Street wharf.

"I want to try this one first," he told Maysie. "Is Poydras Street very far?"

"Don't you worry. We got the car today, so we can go all the way to Pilottown if you want."

Ozzy didn't know where Pilottown was, but he knew that somewhere out there was a ship that would take him to Europe. Someday he would tell a biographer about this day. "I shipped out of New Orleans as a common deck swabber and I still remember the name of the ship: the *Almeria Lykes.*"

Chapter 15

MAYSIE came downstairs wearing a white sweater over a paisley dress. "I'm a little out of fashion," she said. "Last time I wore this was in high school."

"No, you look great."

The dress was short, and when Maysie got in the car, it rode up above her knees. Ozzy had to use all his willpower to keep from staring.

"First thing we do," Maysie said, "is get you some new clothes."

They were driving through narrow tree-lined streets where flickering sunlight turned her hair from brown to copper and back again. Ozzy sniffed his collar. "Do I smell bad?"

"It's not that. It's what you look like."

"You mean scuzzy?"

"I mean all dressed in black like that."

"What's the matter with it?"

"If you don't know, I'm not going to tell you. Except

you look like some low-class drug pusher that nobody would give a used toilet paper, much less a job."

"Hey, come on . . ."

"You don't believe me, just hang around some little kids' playground and see how fast you collect the police."

Ozzy looked at his clothes. "I look like a drug pusher?"

"All you need's a couple of gold chains and some alligator boots."

She took him to Richman Brothers on Canal Street, where Ozzy picked out a khaki work shirt. He would have bought shoes and pants, too, but he was afraid to spend the money. He needed underwear, but he didn't want to buy it with Maysie watching. For a while he delayed at the shirt rack, hoping she'd get bored and go off somewhere. Finally he said, "Maybe you better check on Tilla, okay?"

"Check him? What for?"

"I can't remember if I locked the car or not."

Maysie rolled her eyes. "Ain't nobody going to steal that silly lizard." She crossed her arms and waited. Ozzy took the shirt and they went to the cash register. A clerk rang up the sale and said, "Will that be all?"

"Oh," Ozzy mumbled, "I almost forgot."

He left Maysie standing there and hurried back to the underwear table. The men's briefs were lined up, three in a package. It was the first time he'd been shopping for clothes without Mom, and he wasn't sure of the size. He was still trying to make up his mind when Maysie came up.

"You find the right brand?"

"Oh, sorry."

She craned her neck to see the label. "A Fruit of the Loom man, huh?" Ozzy instinctively tucked the package behind him, and Maysie giggled. "Don't worry, I won't tell nobody your deep, dark secret."

Ozzy didn't know what to say. He wasn't married, so he didn't have any experience kidding around about people's underwear. He gave her a black look and pretended not to know her when he paid for the underwear.

Ozzy had this image of New Orleans with the Mississippi River sliding through town like a silver snake, but that's not how it was. Mostly there were piers and warehouses blocking the view, and in the few places that were open, all you could see was a levee. "We're just a few feet above sea level," Maysie told him. "So without the levee, everything would flood out."

At the Poydras Street wharf, Ozzy stood beside the car and changed his shirt. The air was warm and moist and lay against his chest like somebody breathing. He could see the pilothouse of the *Almeria Lykes* above the warehouse. It was like a white metal veranda with windows set well back under a low roof. Behind the pilothouse there was an oval smokestack showing the Lykes emblem, an *L* framed by a flattened diamond. Ozzy wondered if he'd be looking at the same emblem in Marseilles or Hamburg or Liverpool three weeks from now.

Maysie came up to him. "Remember, if this one don't work, ask them where else to try." She reached around his neck and straightened his collar. It was a simple gesture, one Mom had done a thousand times, and it brought quick tears to his eyes. He looked away, took a deep breath, and the feeling passed.

A crane moved between the warehouse and the ship, lifting huge metal containers from the deck and stacking them like children's alphabet blocks on the pier. Ozzy grabbed the railing and started up a metal gangway. From above him came two alternating sounds, a dull thud and a sharp smack. When he reached the deck, he found a muscular guy in a blue uniform doing push-ups, the kind where you slap your hands together between each one. When he saw Ozzy, he stood up and wiped his hands on his pants.

"Yeah?"

"Hi, uh, is the captain around?"

"Not here." The guy started shaking his arms out like an Olympic swimmer. He was a body-builder type, with a jaw two inches too long and a shirt two sizes too small.

"Well, is there anybody I could talk to about a job?"

"What kind of a job?" He started doing isometrics, clenching his fists one on top of the other and then trying to push them together.

"A cabin boy, a dishwasher, it doesn't matter. I'm willing to do anything."

"Ship's hiring's done at the office."

"What office?"

"Whoever owns the ships."

"Is that Lykes? Is that who owns this one?"

"I guess." He gritted his teeth and made one last effort to mold his hands together. Then he let out a big burst of air and dropped his hands to his sides.

"So where's the office, do you know?"

"Downtown. Big building with the name on it." The guy started rolling his head like a dead weight around in circles.

"Would you happen to have the exact address of the big building downtown?"

"Nope. I'm just security."

You're just an idiot, Ozzy wanted to say. Here he was, making the biggest decision of his life, his date with destiny, and he was stuck talking to an idiot.

"Is there anyone aboard who could tell me where the office is?"

"This guy's on the ship. Ask him."

Ozzy turned around. A thickset man in green overalls was coming up the gangway. The security guy didn't look like he was going to make any introductions, so when the man stepped aboard, Ozzy said, "Excuse me, but do you know where the ship's company offices are located?"

"What do you need?"

"Wants a job," the security guy said before Ozzy could answer. The new man looked at Ozzy, and the deep lines along his forehead grew deeper. He seemed about fifty years old, with crewcut gray hair and kind of a sad, basset-hound expression. "You want a job on ship?"

Ozzy nodded. "Yeah. I'll do anything, as long as I can ship out."

"I don't suppose you've got a card?" His voice was slow and heavy.

"What kind of card?"

"Seaman's certification, issued by the Coast Guard."

"But I just want to be a dishwasher or something."

"Shipboard job, you need a sea cert. Not that it does much good the way things are going these days."

Ozzy felt a vague sense of dread creeping up on him. He should have thought of something like this. He should have known there'd be a bunch of mindless rules and regulations.

"What does it take to get a certification?"

The old man gave him the address of the Coast Guard on something that sounded like Chew-petunias Street. Ozzy had him write it down, and when he showed it to Maysie, she recognized it right away.

"Tchoupitoulas Street? Sure, it's right around the corner."

The Coast Guard station might as well have been a million miles away for all the good it did to go there. First, nobody seemed to know where to go for the certifications. Then, after being sent to three different places, he finally found the right office and they told him to come back after lunch and talk to Chief Braswell. By the time he got back to the car, he was angry.

"Why can't I just get on a ship? Why can't I just find a job and take it? Why does everything always get in the way?"

"Calm down," Maysie said. "We got all afternoon."

"I'm never going to get out of here."

"Sure you will. And if it takes a couple of days longer, you can just stay with us."

"But I want to be gone tomorrow."

"Tomorrow or Thursday or Friday ain't going to make no difference in the long run."

But it did make a difference. When he thought of standing still, of staying in one place, he felt panicky.

Maysie took his arm. "Come on, I know how to cheer you up. We'll get us lunch in the French Quarter."

Chapter 16

THE FRENCH QUARTER was the Paris of his imagination. One minute they were walking down Esplanade Avenue and the next minute they were engulfed in a kaleidoscope of sights and smells and sounds that kept Ozzy turning one way and the other. Two- and three-story pastel buildings crowded close to the street like kids pushing forward to see a parade. The air was fragrant with the smell of flowers and fresh coffee, seafood and spices. A girl in a black velvet evening gown played "Greensleeves" on a violin. A horse-drawn carriage passed, harness bells jingling, yellow-spoked wheels flashing in the sun. Bay windows peeked from brick archways, and everywhere there was iron lacework, wrapping around balconies, racing up posts and columns, spilling over doorways, and casting filigree shadows across the sidewalk.

"It's real," Ozzy kept saying. "It's all real."

"Sure it's real. What'd you think?"

"I mean, Disneyland is real but it's not real. But these

stores actually sell things, and people actually live in those apartments."

Maysie followed his gaze. "I wouldn't mind having me a place like that. I could rent it out and live free the rest of my life."

Ozzy sighed. "It's no wonder people go to French places to live."

Maysie took him to the Court of the Two Sisters. They turned off Royal Street through a wide archway and into a blue-and-white-tiled inner courtyard. As soon as he saw the place, Ozzy knew it was too expensive.

"No, no," Maysie insisted. "My treat. After all, you kept me alive on the way down here."

"But that was only a Big Mac."

"So you can order a Creole Mac."

"They have that?"

"Well, it's called seafood gumbo. Come on."

The place was more like a garden than a restaurant. Flowers overflowed from vases on metal stands and trees leaned out over the tables. In the center was a tiered fountain where water spilled from one level to another and reflected the sunlight against the far wall. Watching his face, Maysie said, "I never seen nobody so crazy about balconies and courtyards."

Ozzy ordered the seafood gumbo, and Maysie got a shrimp salad with a carafe of white wine. He looked at her in surprise. "You have wine for lunch?"

She winked at him. "Must be my Fontaine blood." Then she got up, took her water glass, and poured it out into a flowerpot.

"Why'd you do that?"

"You'll see."

The wine came, and the waitress poured Maysie a glass. After she was gone, Maysie used the empty water glass to pour another, which she handed to him. Ozzy glanced around, but nobody was paying any attention. Maysie raised her glass. "Here's hoping you get the first ship."

After the toast Maysie went to call her mother. As she crossed the courtyard, Ozzy watched the way the shadows flickered over her shoulders and the dress brushed against her legs. He settled back like a king on a throne, lifted his glass, and held it with his little finger raised. If the world could offer him the French Quarter, then all things were possible. The future seemed secure again. He felt better than he had since leaving home. Maybe in his biography he could cheat a little and say he grew up in the French Quarter. He tested the names, whispering them and listening for the right accent. "Rooo Roe-yall."

The waitress brought a thin loaf of warm bread in a wicker basket. Ozzy was buttering the first piece when Maysie came back looking upset. She sat down heavily and reached for her wine.

"What's wrong?"

"He ain't called." She downed the glass in three quick gulps.

"Your husband?"

"That's right. Looks like I screwed things up good this time."

"I thought you didn't want to see him again. I thought that's why you left."

She gave him a long look. "Can I ask you a personal question?"

His senses quickened. A personal question? Was she in love with him? Did she want to know if he was still a virgin? Or was it more stuff about his underwear? He took a sip of wine and kept the glass in front of his face. "What is it you want to know?"

"Well, you remember how I told you Brandt used our house money to buy him a pickup truck? What I done was, I cut him off, and Momma says you just don't do that to a man."

A terrible image formed in his mind. "You cut what off?

Maysie frowned. "Not *what*—him. I cut him off from any loving. See, I warned him, Ozzy. When he started up on this pickup-truck business, I said, 'I don't care if you want to get it, but you take any money from that house account, I'll hold out on you until it gets put back.' And he pouts like a little kid and says, 'Now, babe, don't be like that.' And I says, 'I'm serious, Brandt.' Well, two weeks later he comes in with this big sheepdog grin on his face and says, 'Go look out the window'—like I'm supposed to get excited about this big green pickup in the front yard. 'All right,' I say. 'That's it. No more loving until that bank account gets put back to seven thousand dollars.'" She leaned toward him. "He called my bluff, see?"

Ozzy knew from the way she was looking at him that she wanted him to understand, but he didn't know what to say. He couldn't believe she was telling him all this personal stuff. The waitress brought their food, and Maysie continued the story. At first Brandt had laughed it off. He realized she was serious when she started sleeping on the couch. Then he told her it was illegal for a wife to hold out on her husband, but she showed him a *People* magazine article about the Rideout case, where a woman sued her husband for rape and won. Finally he tried bringing her candy and flowers, but Maysie wouldn't budge. Ozzy wondered how well they really knew each other if Brandt didn't realize how stubborn she was.

Brandt started staying out late. Instead of coming home, he'd hang out at the bar with the single guys on the crew, drinking and shooting pool all night. Maysie kept the dinners warm, but by the time he got home, the food was dried out and Brandt was too drunk to care. One morning she decided to call his bluff. Ozzy noticed she had a thing about calling people's bluffs.

"I said, 'What time you want dinner tonight?' and just like always, he says, 'Whenever I get home.' So I said, 'Dinner's going on the table at seven. If you ain't here by eight, it goes in the trash can.' So sure enough, he don't come back until ten and the first thing he wants is dinner. I brought him the trash bag and put it on the table. 'Dig in,' I says. Well, that done it. He grabs me and says, 'You throw away the dinner, but you ain't going to throw me away.' He drug me into the bedroom and there's no way I could keep him from getting what he wanted. Soon as he fell asleep, that's when I grabbed my fur coat and made it down to the bus station."

Maysie looked down at her salad. She'd already eaten the shrimp, so all she had left was lettuce. Ozzy thought back to when he'd first seen her, two nights ago, in the cold light of the Salina parking lot. He remembered how pretty she looked in her white fur coat. But only an hour before that, she'd been lying naked under some hairy construction guy, who probably grabbed her hips with both hands while they did it. Seeing her now, all sad and worried, made him feel like an older brother. He wanted to reach out and comfort her.

Maysie looked up sheepishly. "Now you know the whole sorry story. Momma says it's my fault for leaving the bed cold. She don't think he'll ever call, and what I started to ask you was, would you call a girl who done like I done or not?"

"I don't know. It would depend on the circumstances, I guess."

"What about the circumstances like I just described? If you were in Brandt's shoes, what would you do?"

If he were in Brandt's shoes? If he were married to Maysie? The thought made him dizzy. Across the table her face seemed to float toward him, her green eyes glistening, her lips moving slightly as she breathed. The wine had gone to his head. He leaned back and laughed nervously.

"I wouldn't want a truck, so you wouldn't have to run away."

"Ozzy, I'm serious."

"Okay, okay." He hunched forward and tried to concentrate. "What is it again? What would I do if I was Brandt and you ran off? I guess, uh, if I loved you, I'd want you back. I mean, I definitely would."

The conversation was getting confusing. *He* wasn't the one in love with Maysie. Was he?

"So what you're saying is, if you had a girl and she

ran off to her mother's and you loved her, you'd call her up."

"I would if it was you."

It was the wrong answer. Maysie's lips quivered and she looked away. "Damn!"

"He doesn't sound good enough for you, anyway."

She looked at him in amazement. "Ozzy, I love him."

"You *love* him?"

" 'Course I love him. What do you think I left him for?"

Now he knew the wine had fuzzed his brain. What she was saying didn't make any sense, but he could see how upset she was, how confused and helpless. He wanted to reach out and help her, to protect her, to hold her.

"Come with me to Paris."

The words flew from his mouth without thinking, but as soon as he said it, he knew it was right. Maysie was pretty, she was fun, and she had guts. She was the most wonderful girl he'd ever known, and he was in love with her. He imagined them living in a tiny garret chiseled out of stone by monks. There would be a narrow window overlooking the Seine, and every morning Maysie would bring him cheese and apples while he wrote. In the afternoon they would go to the Louvre until she was his cultural and intellectual equal. She would learn French without a Southern accent.

"You're crazy," Maysie told him.

"I mean it." He reached across the table and took her hand. "I really like you, Maysie. I want you to come with me."

She looked at him closely and smiled. "You're more

than crazy, you're drunk. And here I am asking *you* for advice."

"No, really, I'll make you famous. I'll write about you like Zelda Fitzgerald, everybody will know what a great person you are—"

She patted his hand as she pulled hers free. "You hush now before you say something that'll turn you red when you remember."

"Why not?"

"Now, don't go pulling faces on me."

"You think I'm kidding."

"I think it's the wine talking, but even if you was in your right mind, it wouldn't work. You want too much for me, Ozzy. That's the type of person you are, a wanter. And Daddy was the same way, only not as smart maybe. I know you think I'm ignorant and stupid—"

"No, I don't."

"Oh, I don't mind, but let me tell you a secret. I got good grades in school whenever I put my mind to it. I could have finished up high and gone to college and learned to talk like a six-o'clock newsman but that's not what I want. What I want is a good man to love and a decent house to live in and some friends I can tell a trouble to when the need comes. I want to raise up my kids so they can look back on being young and say, 'That was a happy time in my life.' Then I want to grow real old and die real fast and I don't care if I never see Paris."

Ozzy didn't know what to say. He tried to remember what they said in *Famous Authorship* about literary destiny and artistic fulfillment, but his mind felt like an overstretched rubber band. Then he remembered something Mom always said. "You know, the unexamined life's not worth living."

Maysie gave him a slow smile. "Ozzy, how'd you get so full of bullshit at such a tender age?"

"It's not bullshit."

"Well, if it sounds like, looks like, smells like—"

"You can't just live like everybody else, believe everything everybody says, do everything everybody else does like some kind of mindless sheep . . ." The words came pouring out, but it was Mom's voice echoing in his mind and somehow he didn't believe what he was saying. He stopped. Maysie was looking at him with her head cocked to one side.

"What are you so mad about?"

"I'm not mad, I'm just . . . I don't want to be . . . you know."

"What?"

"Like everybody else."

"You mean two legs, two arms, and a head?"

"I mean average."

"Average."

"Because most people live lives of quiet—"

Desperation, he was about to say. But he didn't believe it. At least not the way it sounded. Most people seemed happy sometimes and sad sometimes and kind of in between most of the time. He shook his head to try and clear it.

"Ooooh, ooooh," Maysie said. "I know what you need." She turned and waved at the waitress. "Yoo-hoo, miss. We need us some coffee over here, and yesterday would be too late."

"I'm okay," Ozzy grumbled. But the world had taken a little sidestep on him, and he was still trying to regain his balance.

Chapter 17

OZZY was still feeling light-headed when he went to see Chief Braswell. It wasn't the wine, it was the image he had of himself as a famous writer. When he tried to focus on it, all he could see was a kid from Colorado walking into a Coast Guard station. He took a deep breath to build his confidence and walked upstairs to room 216.

Chief Braswell was a short, stocky man with a lumpy nose. He dug around in a file cabinet and brought out a two-page application form. "Here you go, son. Fill this out and bring it back with three wallet-size photos and a passport or birth certificate."

"A birth certificate?"

"Passport or birth certificate, either one."

"What about a driver's license? Isn't that okay?"

"Need a birth certificate. You must have one somewhere."

"I don't. I mean I do, but not with me. I don't live here. I just came to get a job on a ship."

"Son, there's no guarantee you can find a berth even after you get your certification. Jobs just aren't that plentiful these days, but if you want to try you'll need that birth certificate."

Ozzy felt like he'd been kicked in the stomach. His birth certificate. Why hadn't he thought of it? Somehow in the back of his mind he thought if you were on an American ship, it was the same as being on American soil, and if you didn't go ashore, you wouldn't need things like birth certificates or passports. And then, some dark night in Marseilles, he'd drop over the side . . .

No. The image of himself sneaking over the side of a ship wouldn't hold. It was stupid. The whole plan, from beginning to end, was stupid. He walked out of the station in a daze. Instead of going back to the car, he kept walking blindly while everything he'd done, everything he'd thought and believed and hoped for came crumbling down around him.

Maysie called, but he didn't pay any attention. He crossed a ramp that led to a walkway along the levee. Rocks and boulders stretched for twenty feet down to the river. He sat down heavily and rested his head in his hands while the memories came flooding back . . .

"Let's invent a new color," she said once and then spent half a day with him trying to find one. She took Grandpa's wheelchair to the bank so she could sit instead of stand in line. She found an old mannequin at the Salvation Army and stuck it in the bathroom with a toothbrush in its hand. She used to grab Ozzy by the shoulders and whisper, "Let's put a little drama in life!"

And when the discussion came to dying, she said, "I don't want to be buried. Just ride a white horse and cast my ashes from the mountains at dawn." And her eyes would shine and she'd look around to see who was watching. A little drama in life.

"Ozzy?" Maysie sat down beside him. "What is it? What's wrong?"

He shook his head. Maysie put her arm around him, and suddenly there were tears, welling forth from deep inside, wracking his body with sobs.

"Oh, Ozzy, Ozzy," she whispered.

She pulled him close, and he buried his head on her shoulder. Mom was gone. He had lost her twice, first in the mountains and now in his imagination. As she became real to him, her death became real and the grief was more than he could bear.

Later, when his heart was still, he told Maysie what he hadn't told her before—that he was supposed to go with the family to get the Christmas tree. He had gone the year before. He had driven the car the year before, too, just as he would have this year.

"I blamed Dad, but it was me. I should have been there. I could have saved her."

"You don't know that."

"I would have gotten the car. I know I would have." He stared at the dark river, swirling and folding in on itself. "What am I going to do?"

"Same as all of us," Maysie said softly. "Whatever you can."

THEY DROVE BACK to Felicity Lodge, and when they turned the last corner, Maysie let out a gasp. "My God, it's him."

Parked on the street was a mud-spattered green pickup. It was the high kind of workhorse truck where the body looks like it's floating above the wheels. As they pulled into the driveway, Ozzy could see words on the door: *B. Perlmutter.* They were individual stick-on letters, black on a shiny gold background.

"He come all that way," Maysie cried. "I don't believe it." She was half out the door before she remembered. "The ring! The ring!"

"What?"

"Quick, Ozzy, gimme back my double diamond."

Ozzy dug through his pocket and handed it to her. He had never seen her so excited. She ran toward the house, and a man with jet-black hair came down from the porch to meet her. Maysie threw herself into his arms, and he lifted her and carried her into the house. Three old ladies sitting on the porch turned their heads in unison as they passed.

Ozzy got out of the car and went inside. Mrs. Fontaine was standing with Sonny and Sandy at the bottom of the staircase, all of them looking up where Brandt and Maysie had disappeared. When she saw Ozzy, Mrs. Fontaine straightened up and pulled the kids away.

"Sonny, Sandy, y'all go outside and play. Go on, now." Then she turned to Ozzy. "We got us a little excitement, as I guess you noticed. Can I offer you some lemonade in the parlor?"

"First I need to use the phone."

He called collect, and Lance answered. "Where are you, man? Everybody's been crazy."

"I'm in New Orleans."

"You're kidding."

"How is everybody? How's Dad?"

"How do you think? He's been up all night, the cops have been here—I had to hide in the basement, man. I mean it was—hold on." There was a muffled conversation, and then Aunt Rose came on.

"Ozzy, what happened? Where have you been?"

"I've been traveling. Let me talk to Dad, okay?"

"Ozzy, if you knew the pain you caused. And not just for your father, for everybody. Sissy, Lance, myself, we've been searching the streets and sitting by the phone, talking to the police, calling neighbors. You have no idea what you've done to everybody . . ." She ran out of breath and paused. "Ozzy?"

"Can I speak to Dad, please?"

"Well I . . . I just mean . . . we were so worried . . ."

"I know, Aunt Rose. Can I talk to Dad now?"

She left, and Ozzy felt a new sense of control. It was so much easier when you looked at things straight on.

"Ozzy?"

"Hi, Dad."

"Thank God, thank God." His voice wavered. "I thought I'd lost you, too."

"I know. I'm sorry."

"Where are you? Are you all right?"

"I'm fine, but I just . . . I feel bad about what I said. About Mom and all."

There was a pause, then Dad said slowly, "She was her own person, Ozzy."

"I know."

"I loved her with all my heart but . . . I couldn't control her. Nobody ever could."

"Dad, I want to come home."

BRANDT AND MAYSIE offered to take him to the airport. While Brandt cleaned out the truck, Maysie told him what happened. "Do you believe he made that whole long drive in fifteen straight hours? Didn't stop but once for gas and to pee. That old truck's got an extra gas tank, that's how he done it so quick."

Maysie and Brandt had agreed on a new plan. From now on the house account would be under Maysie's name, so Brandt couldn't get his hands on the money no matter what kind of truck-buying impulses came over him. "See, Ozzy? That shows how much he loves me."

Ozzy smiled and said nothing. What she had said earlier was true, they were from different worlds. But there was a certain something when he'd first seen her at bus station and later in the Court of the Two Sisters . . .

He gave Tilla to Sonny, who promised to catch a hundred flies a day for the chameleon. At the airport Brandt and Maysie waited with him in line to buy a ticket.

"Y'all be sure and write," Maysie told him. "Here, where's that notebook you're always writing things down in?"

He gave it to her, and she wrote their address while Brandt talked to him about water towers. Brandt was thin in the waist and hips but had a muscular chest and thick forearms. He was actually a handsome enough guy with his jet-black hair and eyebrows and big, wide smile. He offered to help Ozzy get a water tower job in the summer.

"You can clear a good twenty bucks an hour."

"And you can keep it," Maysie said, "if you don't go buying no pickup trucks."

"Just get yourself a mule-headed woman and you won't have no money to spend, anyway."

Maysie bumped him with her hip, and Brandt grabbed her around the waist. They were touching each other every chance they got. At the boarding gate Brandt gave him a firm handshake and Maysie brought out a white envelope. "Here's a little souvenir of New Orleans." She tucked it into his jacket pocket and gave him a big hug. "You take care, now."

Ozzy wanted to say something to tell her how he felt and how much it meant meeting her, but he didn't quite know how. It would take time to find the right words; he didn't have to be a writer to know that.

He boarded the plane and as soon as he was seated, he pulled out the envelope and opened it. Inside was a twenty-dollar bill and a color postcard of the Court of the Two Sisters. He turned it over. The message was written in pink lipstick, the imprint of her lips. A man in the seat beside him glanced over.

"Got a girl in New Orleans?"

He turned the postcard over and shook his head. "Maybe someday . . ."

The plane began to move, and Ozzy Mills was on his way home.

About the Author

R. E. ALLEN has worked as a flight instructor, script-writer, and film editor. He served as president of the Berkeley Film Institute and once spent six months in Zimbabwe guarding a gold mine. Currently he lives in New York.

R. E. Allen was the recipient of a National Endowment for the Arts grant, and has published two novels for adults. He was selected for a Doubleday-Columbia Fellowship. *Ozzy on the Outside* won the Sixth Annual Delacorte Press Prize for an Outstanding First Young Adult Novel.